## "I ne

Juliet watched Bra... ...her and then back... ...is your mother?"

"Yes. That was taken before I was born."

"Wow, you *do* look a lot like her. And the man is..."

Refocusing her attention on the picture, Juliet said, "That's what I need to find out."

Brandon's gaze searched her face. "Why?"

She chewed on her bottom lip as she debated telling him the whole sordid truth. Having a friend to confide in and help her process what she knew sounded wonderful.

But was Brandon that person? Could she trust him completely?

"I want to find this man to see if he knows anything about her disappearance and–" her voice caught "–and what exactly his relationship was to my married mother."

* * *

## Books by Terri Reed

Love Inspired Suspense

*Strictly Confidential* #21
*Double Deception* #41
*Beloved Enemy* #44

Love Inspired

*Love Comes Home* #258
*A Sheltering Love* #302
*A Sheltering Heart* #362
*A Time of Hope* #370

## TERRI REED

grew up in a small town nestled in the foothills of the Sierra Nevada. To entertain herself, she created stories in her head, and when she put those stories to paper her teachers in grade school, high school and college encouraged her imagination. Living in Italy as an exchange student whetted her appetite for travel, and modeling in New York, Chicago and San Francisco gave her a love for the big city, as well. She has also coached gymnastics and taught in a preschool. She enjoys walks on the beach, hikes in the mountains and exploring cities. From a young age she attended church, but it wasn't until her thirties that she really understood the meaning of a faith-filled life. Now living in Portland, Oregon, with her college-sweetheart husband, two wonderful children, a rambunctious Australian shepherd and a fat guinea pig, she feels blessed to be able to share her stories and her faith with the world. She loves to hear from readers at P.O. Box 19555, Portland, OR 97280.

# TERRI REED

# Beloved Enemy

Steeple
Hill®

Published by Steeple Hill Books™

Special thanks and acknowledgment are given
to Terri Reed for her contribution to
THE SECRETS OF STONELEY miniseries.

Many thanks to my fellow Stoneley authors:
Lenora, Shirlee, Irene, Val and Lynn. You made this fun!

Special thanks to Diane Dietz and everyone
at Steeple Hill Books for giving me
Juliet and Brandon to play with.
I enjoyed them.

STEEPLE HILL BOOKS

Steeple
Hill®

ISBN-13: 978-0-373-44234-8
ISBN-10:   0-373-44234-3

BELOVED ENEMY

www.SteepleHill.com

**Printed in U.S.A.**

Beloved, let us love one another, for love is of God;
and everyone who loves is born of God
and knows God.

—*1 John* 4:7

Thou art thy mother's glass, and she in thee
Calls back the lovely April of her prime.
—William Shakespeare
"Sonnet 3," lines 10–11

# ONE

Juliet Blanchard adjusted the dress on the fidgety model, making sure all the angles and lines were shown to the best advantage before shooing the girl out onto the runway set up in the middle of the convention center. Thankfully, the mild Vermont fall weather was drawing in a big crowd for tonight's event.

Blowing a wisp of blond hair out of her eyes and taking a place near the stage behind the curtain, Juliet watched the crowd's reaction with pleasure. This was her last show with the Vermont State University's Fashion Design program before graduation in January. Sitting among the crowd were design house representatives hoping to recruit the newest and brightest upcoming designers to their respective design houses.

She would not be one of those recruits.

Juliet tried to squelch the rising disappointment that threatened to choke her. She'd promised her family she'd come to work in the family business after graduation.

But someday she would strike out on her own and make a name for herself as a fashion designer.

Her attention snagged on a tall man standing at the back of the crowd. She guessed he was mid- to late twenties. His wavy, dark-blond hair was just long enough to be considered rebellious yet fashionable. And his dark eyes seemed to be staring straight at her.

She knew there was no way he could see her through the glare of the hot spotlights aimed at the stage, but still, awareness sent tingles over her arms. She'd seen this man at the last four shows. Was he with a fashion house, or the friend of a classmate?

The model returned and Juliet refocused her attention on the clothes. She couldn't afford to let her mind become distracted by anything or anyone. Too much work lay ahead of her before she made the move to Blanchard Fabrics and too many issues with her family remained unresolved.

Backstage, she helped the model change and then carefully handed the clothing to her assistant to be put on a mannequin for the viewing after the show.

"Juliet, come on," Giles Manfred called as he hustled his students onstage for introductions. Juliet reluctantly went. She didn't have anyone in the crowd cheering for her. Her five sisters were all busy with their own lives and her father wouldn't have come, even if she'd asked.

Onstage Juliet accepted the applause for what it was: an acknowledgement of her designs. She felt gratified to know her work was well received.

A movement on the audience floor to her right caught her attention. Mr. Tall, Blond and Yummy had weaved his way through the crowd, halting at the foot of the stage steps. The cutting-edge styling of the olive-colored suit fit his broad shoulders and long, lean legs to perfection. Juliet tilted her head in silent question as his warm brown eyes studied her intently. The man inclined his head in acknowledgement.

Intrigued, Juliet smiled. What was up with this guy?

Shaking away the question, she moved down the steps. The man shifted forward. His warm hand cupped her elbow as she descended. She drew back slightly.

"Do I know you?" she asked over the din of excited voices.

With a slight pressure to her elbow, he propelled her through the throng of people to the back edge of the crowd where the noise level dropped significantly.

"No, you don't know me. But I know who you are, Juliet. And I'm very impressed with your designs."

The combination of his deep voice and his praise sent pleasure and pride sliding over her skin. "Thank you. Can I ask what brings you here?"

He gave her a boyish grin that set her heart pounding. "You can. And I'd love to tell you about the connections I have in Paris. But I'd like to tell you over dinner."

Dinner? With a stranger? She could just hear her eldest sister, Miranda's, shocked *tsk* echoing in her head.

"I really don't think that would be appropriate, considering I don't even know your name," Juliet replied.

Mr. Tall, Blond and Yummy stuck out his hand. "Brandon De Witte."

She shook his hand, setting off a firestorm of sparks shooting up her arm. "Juliet Blanchard. But you already know that. So, why me?"

One side of his generous mouth curved upward. "Come to dinner with me and I'll tell you."

She extracted her hand and shook her head, ready again to explain why that was impossible.

He held up a hand to stop her from speaking. "We'll be in a public restaurant. What can happen?"

"People might talk," she countered, even though the excuse sounded lame.

He made a face. "Who and to whom?"

Obviously he didn't really know who the Blanchards were or he wouldn't ask. She'd chosen a school far enough away from anyone remotely connected to her family that gossip very rarely reached her sisters' or her father's ears. Unlike when Juliet was in high school.

Back then she couldn't make a move, no matter how innocent or rebellious, without someone informing her siblings. Being the youngest of five successful sisters, Juliet had a lot to live up to. Striving to prove herself capable in a family of overachievers kept Juliet busy most of the time.

But here was this handsome—she glanced at his ring finger and was glad to see no shiny gold band—seemingly unattached man asking to take her to dinner in a public setting. What harm could come from accepting the invitation?

And while working in Paris had to stay a dream for now, getting to know someone with connections there wasn't a bad idea. As she'd heard her father say often, look ahead to the future if you want to accomplish anything.

"All right," she said, deciding that tonight she'd let the untamed streak inside her rule. "Let me grab my purse."

She hurried backstage to locate her purse and coat. On the way back out, Giles stopped her. His rotund body blocked the exit.

"Where are we off to?" her instructor asked.

"Dinner with a…friend."

A sly gleam entered Giles's gray eyes. "With the man I saw you talking to? Hmm. Interesting."

Heat crept up Juliet's neck. "It's just dinner. Nothing romantic."

"Right." Giles nodded sagely.

"The show went great," Juliet said to change the focus.

Giles clapped his hands together. "Exceptionally! Your designs specifically were touted as the best. I really wish you'd reconsider taking that job at your family's factory. Darling, you are so much better than a factory worker."

Juliet refrained from rolling her eyes. "I'll be heading the marketing department."

"Honey, you're a designer, not some pencil pusher!"

"I have a minor in marketing, Giles," she pointed out for the umpteenth time.

He made a scoffing sound.

She laughed. "I've got to run. I'll see you on Monday."

"Have fun," he called out to her as she hurried back to where she'd left Mr. De Witte.

"Ready?" He held out his arm.

She linked hers through, conscious of the strong muscles beneath his sleeve. "Where are we going?"

"Do you like Italian food?"

"Love it."

"Great. Fratelli's right next door it is then."

A few minutes later, they were seated by a large plate glass window overlooking Lake Champlain. The moon hung low in the clear fall night sky and cast a luminescent glow across the water's surface. Twinkling lights marked the homes along the shoreline.

A waiter approached, took their orders and left. In the background above the soft clinking of dinnerware and low conversations, the music of Vivaldi played.

Juliet twirled the mineral water in her goblet. "Are you a local?"

"No. I'm in town to study a few companies that I'm interested in."

"Companies? What do you do?" She took a sip of the water.

"I find companies that are struggling and either buy them or revitalize them."

"Ah, a corporate raider."

He gave a careless shrug. "That's a misnomer."

"So you said you'd tell me what brought you to our fashion show. And about your connections in Paris."

"Your designs brought me to the show."

She blinked, flattered. "How did you—"

"I saw the spread in the *Vermont News* about the school and the show listings."

The article that had appeared at the beginning of the fall term had featured two of her earlier pieces as well as a picture of the graduating class. Her father had been less than pleased. He didn't like having the Blanchard name bandied about in such a way. His reaction still stung.

"I have a strong contact in the House of Roan in Paris. I would be more than willing to introduce you. You have heard of Roan, haven't you?" he asked.

"Of course. Who hasn't? He's only the leading, most over-the-top designer in the world." Even the suggestion that she could set a foot in the House of Roan would be beyond her wildest imaginations.

"You would love working in Paris," he continued. "The Seine and the Louvre. The cafés and the history."

She stifled a sigh. Her dream of one day living and working in the City of Lights would have to wait until she fulfilled her promise to her family. She didn't want to let herself entertain the crazy thought of designing for Roan. Better to face her reality and be content than set herself up for disappointment. "That is so kind of you to offer. What do you get out of it?"

"Wow. You don't pull any punches, do you?"

He didn't look offended, which she found refreshing. Too often people didn't take well to the direct approach. Her family surely didn't. She'd learned to filter her thoughts growing up. But in the real world, she found straightforwardness more effective. "I have to wonder why the interest. You seem to be a man who wouldn't offer to help for purely altruistic purposes."

He placed a hand over his heart. "You wound me."

The twinkle in his eye contradicted his words.

"I think not," she replied with a smile.

He leaned forward, his expression turning earnest. "You have extraordinary vision. A talent that should be encouraged and fostered."

She swallowed back the sudden lump in her throat. If only her family thought the same way. "I appreciate your confidence. Now, tell me, where did you get that fabulous suit?"

He sat back and thankfully took the hint that she wanted to change the subject. They talked fashion and finances, art and sports. When the conversation turned to faith, he'd stiffened and she had the distinct impression by the bitter tone in his voice that something dark lurked in his past that kept him from God. That made her sad. Her own past was fraught with drama and heartache, but her faith had been the anchor in her life.

"Where did you grow up?" she asked.

"In Bangor."

"Are your parents still there?"

A sorrowful look entered his eyes. "No. My parents died in a car accident many years ago."

"I'm so sorry."

He quickly veered the conversation to other

topics including her family and the factory. He asked question after question about her life in Stoneley, about her siblings and her father. She actually enjoyed regaling him with stories of her more colorful exploits as a child and a teen. She was amazed to discover the time passing without the awkward silences that usually transpired on dates.

But this wasn't a traditional date, she reminded herself later that evening when he walked her to her car. "Thank you, Brandon. I really had a nice time," she said as she opened the driver's side door.

And she had. More so than she had in a very long time. She liked this man. Too bad she didn't have room in her life at the moment for a relationship.

"I did, too. You're a very interesting woman. And I hope you will let me know if I can set you up with my contact in Paris. I know the House of Roan would flip to have someone of your caliber." He pulled a card from the inside pocket of his suit jacket. "Here's my card. Call me if you decide to take me up on my offer."

Beneath the warm glow of the parking lot light, she studied the card. His name and a number were the only information printed in black lettering on the pale blue face.

"Juliet?"

She lifted her gaze and her breath stalled somewhere between her heart and her throat. The way he was looking at her, as if he were memorizing every curve and line of her face, was as intoxicating as if he were touching her. She swallowed. Her whole being tingled with anticipation and a powerful yearning she felt helpless against.

His head dipped until his lips hovered over hers, waiting, inviting. His hesitation was so sweet and so alluring. He was making it clear he wouldn't proceed without her permission.

Why not? What harm could come from one kiss?

Standing on tiptoe, she closed the distance. Their lips touched. His were firm, yet molding to hers effortlessly. A delicious sensation coursed over her, melting her bones and turning her to mush.

Sure that at any moment her legs would give out, she clasped his arms. His big, strong hands closed around her and slowly eased her back. He gentled the kiss and slid his mouth across her jaw to just below her ear.

"Good night, Juliet," he whispered as he disengaged from her, steadying her. "'Parting is such sweet sorrow.'" He smiled then turned to leave.

Leaning against the car with a dreamy sigh, she watched him walk away. She bit her lip to keep from calling him back. She wasn't ready for him to leave, but she knew she couldn't ask him to stay. Yes, he'd made her feel special, and yes, she was attracted to him, but both were temporary.

She had a goal, a focus, and it certainly didn't

include a romance. Proving herself capable had to stay her priority.

And no matter what, she would ignore the wistful voice in her head that hoped she'd see Brandon De Witte again one day.

Talk about a dark and stormy night, Juliet thought as she pulled up to the ornate iron gate of Blanchard Manor. Perched high on the cliffs overlooking the Atlantic Ocean just outside of Stoneley, Maine, the huge, ominous house seemed to have been built for nights such as this. She lowered the window and leaned out of her orange Honda Element to reach the security keypad.

A blast of icy March wind and sleet hit her face, stinging her eyes and whipping her hair in a frenzied dance. Her gloved hands fumbled on the pad. With a frustrated yank, she ripped off her right glove and tried again. While fighting against the stiffness the cold air caused in her fingers, she finally managed to punch in her code to release the gate.

Shivering, she powered the window up and waited for the slow-moving hunk of metal to get out of the way. Before the gate was fully opened, she sped through the gap, her tires spinning slightly on the slick agate pavement.

The long, winding drive up the hill usually provided a lush and beautiful view of the gardens through the trees. On clear days, glimpses of the ocean beyond the cliffs were breathtaking.

However, on this cold winter night, all Juliet could see were the looming shadows of the trees and the large stone manor house rising up ahead like some unearthly specter waiting for its next victim.

She swallowed back the trepidation that had been looming over her for months now, ever since Leo Santiago had given her sister Bianca the picture of their late mother, dated *after* her death. That one act had set in motion a series of devastating events.

Bianca was convinced their mother, who supposedly died not long after Juliet was born, was really alive. Bianca had hired a private investigator to track Mother down, but he had died under suspicious circumstances. Juliet shivered even though the heat in the car was cranked on high. Inside the house her sisters waited for her with more information that they'd uncovered.

Juliet wasn't sure she wanted to know. Part of her was scared to let her hopes rise, because if their mother was alive, then the question became why did she abandon them?

A secret guilt lived deep inside of Juliet's soul. She knew that their mother disappeared because of her. If she hadn't been born, then Trudy Blanchard wouldn't have slid into postpartum depression and left.

Juliet pulled around the circular drive to the garages on the side of the manor. Popping open the glove box, she hit the button on the little black garage opener tucked inside the compartment. The third door of the six garages slid upward. Juliet pulled in behind her sister Portia's vintage VW Bug. Her father's Jaguar and the two black Town Cars were in their customary places.

The parking spots where Bianca's silver sports car and Rissa's dark blue Porsche were usually parked when the girls came home were conspicuously empty. They'd probably taken commuter flights instead of driving in because of the weather.

Bianca lived and worked in Boston and Rissa resided in Manhattan. Both women were successful in their chosen fields; Bianca was a trial lawyer and Rissa a playwright. Portia was successful, as well, with her arts-and-crafts shop. And Miranda, who still lived at the manor, wrote poetry and produced unique, handmade books. Juliet's other sister, Delia, had gone off to college in Hawaii and only occasionally returned. Delia owned and operated a surf shop on the beach.

At twenty-three, Juliet was the only one without a career. This was why her family pressured her to agree to work at Blanchard Fabrics. At least she'd have some work experience to put on a résumé, her sister Bianca had stated as a way to mollify her reluctance.

But the reason Juliet committed to the promise was because it had seemed important to their father, a cold and distant man whose love and approval Juliet coveted, but hadn't yet obtained.

She hoped by being the one daughter to actually work in the company, her father might finally see her capabilities and show her some respect. And for once she'd have some of his undivided attention by working with him at the factory. So she'd put her own newly found dream of fashion design on hold and had come home.

The garage door rumbled shut behind the car as Juliet grabbed her bags. She'd already had the rest of her personal belongings shipped home. She assumed the housekeeper, Sonya Garcia, would have had everything unpacked and put away by now. Sonya kept a very tidy house and was very strict with the girls. Juliet had a small trinket tucked away in her bag for Sonya, as well as one for Juliet's spinster aunt, Winnie.

Juliet paused at the door leading into the house. Once she walked in through that door, there would be no going back. She would be fully committed to her promise to start working at Blanchard Fabrics and being embroiled in whatever new drama unfolded concerning their mother.

And their father.

# TWO

Juliet took a moment to still her thoughts, praying out loud, "Lord, You are in control and I trust You. Bless me with Your presence and let Your will be done in my life."

On a deep breath, she opened the door and stepped into the mudroom, though she doubted the tiled floor and porcelain sink had seen much mud since she'd left home at seventeen. She smiled to see her fuzzy tiger-print slippers waiting for her by the door that would take her into the hall of the main floor.

Kicking off her big, clunky boots, she slipped her feet into her slippers and then shuffled into the body of the house. She passed through the stainless steel, state-of-the-art kitchen where the chef and his assistant were busy preparing the evening meal. The smells of spices and savory roasted meat teased her senses and she dropped her bags to see what samples she could snag.

"Ah, Miss Juliet, you are home," the chef, Andre,

boomed before wrapping her in a quick bear hug. Andre had been with the Blanchards for more than a decade and had overseen the remodel that had updated the kitchen.

"What are we having tonight?" she asked, peering into the simmering pots.

"Lamb, herbed rice, winter vegetables and fresh bread," Andre replied as he resumed his culinary work.

Marco, the newest assistant in a long line of assistants, waved Juliet over. He'd befriended Juliet months earlier when he'd discovered her weakness for desserts. He uncovered a tray piled high with powdered squares. "Lemon bars," he said and nodded with his head for her to take one.

Mouthing a silent *oh,* Juliet snagged one from the top and popped the whole square in her mouth. She closed her eyes in delight as the sweet and tart flavors burst against her taste buds. She gave Marco a thumbs-up before grabbing her bags and continuing on through the house.

Every time Juliet came home she was struck by the majesty and castlelike interior of the huge stone mansion, especially the foyer. Dark and forbidding, like some medieval fortress. The huge, round mahogany table, decorated with a large, sparkling crystal vase full of brightly colored, specially grown flowers, sat center stage.

But it was the sweeping walnut staircase that

brought a smile to Juliet's lips as she remembered sliding down the wide, ornate banisters. She and her sister Delia would have such fun zooming down and then racing up the stairs. Their father had hated when they acted like tomboys. Juliet had learned to wait until her father left the house before having her fun.

Now Juliet vaulted, as best she could in her fuzzy slippers, up the stairs, eager to get to her room before facing her siblings. She could hear them gathered in the parlor to the right of the staircase. The echo of their voices followed her, pricking her conscience with guilt for not immediately saying hello to them.

She made it undetected to her bedroom. Airy and light with splashes of color, the room was a welcome relief to the darkness of the rest of the house.

She quickly unpacked and freshened up. The drive from Vermont had been long and especially tiring on such a stormy night. A quiet knock on the door made her cringe. Busted.

She opened the door to find her aunt, Winnie, standing in the hall. Her faded red hair was up in her usual chignon and her warm hazel eyes regarded Juliet with affection.

"Hi, Auntie," Juliet said as they embraced.

"I was checking on dinner and Andre mentioned you were home." Winnie held Juliet at arm's length. "Why are you sneaking around? Your sisters and I have been anxiously waiting to see you."

"I know. I just needed a moment to get settled, that's all." Juliet shrugged

Winnie hugged her again. "Of course, dear. I understand. Now, let's join your sisters for a few moments before dinner is served."

Arm in arm, Juliet and Winnie descended the stairs. At the parlor door, Juliet paused as Winnie stepped in. Love and pride for her siblings filled Juliet's heart, replacing the earlier need for a quiet moment. Each one was dear and special. And, like herself, named after one of Shakespeare's heroines. Juliet would do anything to make them happy.

"Juliet!" exclaimed Bianca, who rushed forward to squeeze her tightly. Bianca's straight, dark hair brushed over her tailored suit.

"Welcome home, sis," called Portia from where she sat on the floor near the fireplace. Beside her, Portia's twin sister, Nerissa, whom they called Rissa for short, blew Juliet a kiss. A board game lay between the twins. Most likely to distract themselves from the storm brewing outside.

Juliet had always envied the twins' long, dark curls and petite frames. They were exact images of each other and extremely beautiful. They had a special bond that none of the other sisters could enter into and that made Juliet feel even more the outsider.

Her eldest sister, Miranda, sat on the settee with an afghan wrapped about her shoulders. Her wavy brown hair was pulled back in a twist, emphasizing her delicate features. Her golden-brown eyes stared at Juliet with concern. "I was getting worried, with the storm and all."

With an arm around Bianca's waist, Juliet moved into the room. "I made it just fine, Miranda. How are *you* doing?"

"Better now that everyone is here," Miranda said softly.

Juliet accepted the answer even though they all knew Miranda had dodged the real issue. For years Miranda had suffered from a mild case of agoraphobia, which kept her from moving away from the manor. And, like her other sisters, Miranda hated storms.

Winnie took a seat next to Miranda. Bianca led Juliet to the second settee that faced the other two ladies. Portia and Rissa abandoned their game to move closer.

"I wish Delia were here," Juliet said softly. She could see the same sentiment in the eyes of each sister. Thankfully last month, Delia, short for Cordelia, had come home for the Winter Festival, an annual event that none of the girls would ever miss. But Delia's absence now left the circle of sisters incomplete.

"We'll call her later," Bianca stated in her brisk way and patted Juliet's hand.

Grateful to the sister who had stepped in to be her mentor and protector, Juliet gave Bianca a smile. For a moment all the women sat in silence, and Juliet wondered if they, too, were reluctant to talk about their mother.

Growing up in this house, the girls were all forbidden to breathe their mother's name, let alone ask questions of their father about her. Only Aunt Winnie kept their mother alive in their hearts with stories of her, unbeknownst to their father.

That same oppressive silence threatened to keep them all from speaking now.

Forging ahead to get the inevitable over with, Juliet said, "So. From the last conversation we had on the phone, I take it there is more news."

"Portia, why don't you fill Juliet in," Bianca said.

Portia nodded. "Mick uncovered paperwork that shows when Grandfather retired from the company and named Father CEO, Father, in turn, named all of us as heirs to his majority stock shares."

Juliet let the meaning of Portia's words sink in. "Me, too?"

Portia's dark eyebrows drew together. "Of course, you, too. All of us would have equal share in the company."

For Juliet, this news was welcome. That their father would include her with the others as his heirs said at least he didn't hate her. She wouldn't go so far as to say he loved her. Ronald Blanchard wasn't big on affectionate demonstrations, at least with his daughters, Juliet in particular.

For some reason, one Juliet suspected she knew, Ronald kept a physical as well as emotional distance from his youngest child. Juliet assumed it was because, unlike the other girls, her looks favored their mother. She was the oddball and always felt a bit out of place among the other dark-haired, dark-eyed girls.

"That's great." Juliet turned her gaze to Aunt Winnie, their father's only sibling, who sat quietly beside Miranda with her hands folded primly in her lap. The exact details of the news struck Juliet. "But what about Aunt Winnie? Why wouldn't she be included? That stinks."

Winnie looked up, affection for her niece shining bright in her hazel eyes. "I'm sure Father and Ronald know what's best."

Juliet exchanged a glance with Portia, who rolled her eyes at her aunt's statement.

Rissa spoke up. "I wouldn't be too sure of that. Not after what we found out about how Grandfather took ownership of the factory."

All the girls nodded in agreement. It had been a blow to learn that their grandfather hadn't built Blanchard Fabrics from the ground up as they'd all been told. Howard Blanchard had used some less than ethical tactics to acquire the factory from a man named Lester Connolly.

Grandfather and Lester Connolly apparently once loved the same woman, who chose Lester over

Howard. In retaliation, Howard went after the man's company. The whole ordeal was much too sordid and embarrassing to think about. Especially now with Grandfather's Alzheimer's advancing so rapidly.

Juliet suppressed a shudder. She prayed that neither she nor her sisters would be afflicted with the dreaded disease in the future. It was so hard watching a vibrant man decline.

Juliet turned her gaze to Bianca. "Is there anything we can do to include Aunt Winnie?"

Bianca frowned. "I don't know. I'll have to check into it."

"You'd better tell her the rest," Mirada prodded.

Bianca gave her hand a squeeze. "There's more." She looked to Portia. "Portia?"

Juliet braced herself as she turned her attention back to Portia.

Portia's dark eyes were filled with an intensity that made the hair at Juliet's nape stand on end. "Mick also recently discovered a document with our mother's signature on it. The paper was dated a year after her supposed death and gave Father full custodial rights to all of us."

A sharp thudding started behind Juliet's left temple. She tried to rein in the anxious flutter of dread that took flight in her stomach. "First that picture dated after Mother's death and now a document dated after her death? How can this be?"

"Apparently Daddy lied to us," Miranda stated, her complexion going even paler.

"Apparently," Juliet repeated dryly. Of Bianca, she asked, "Have you authenticated the document?"

Bianca nodded. "It's legal. Assuming it's our mother's signature," she added. "We've sent it to a lab that specializes in verifying signatures. We should know soon."

"It might not be her signature, right? Just like the photo Leo gave you. The date could be wrong. Both could be some kind of sick joke or a mistake."

Juliet saw the flash of hurt in Bianca's eyes. Leo Santiago and Bianca were dating now, even though Leo had been working for their father with orders to bring Bianca into the family business. He'd quit working for Ronald because he didn't like being manipulated, especially since he fell in love with Bianca. He'd even moved to Boston to be near Bianca.

"I'm sorry, Bianca. I can't help being skeptical about the date written on the back of the photo. That could have been written at any time by anyone. Just because the date is after Mother's death, doesn't prove she's alive. Neither does this latest piece of 'evidence.'"

"You know I discovered that Mother may have been at the sanitarium in Chicago," Bianca said grimly.

Juliet cringed. "I know nothing of the sort. You didn't find *her.* All you found were more questions, more dead ends and nothing but false hope."

Rissa jumped to her feet. "Juliet, how can you be so mean?"

Portia rose, as well. "Come on, Juliet, you have to see that things don't add up."

Juliet shook her head. "I'm not trying to be mean, Rissa. And you're right, Portia, things don't add up." She shifted her gaze to Bianca, hating the tears she saw shimmering in her eyes. "I just don't want more pain. For any of us."

It had been agonizing growing up under the dark cloud of their mother's abandonment and death. To be stirring up the old fears and hurts now couldn't be good for any of them.

In a steady voice, Bianca stated, "I'm sure in my heart that our mother is alive and I plan to keep trying to find her."

And she would keep at it, Juliet had no doubts. "But at what cost?"

She could see that Bianca understood her meaning. Emotionally this quest would have a high price tag.

Aunt Winnie pleaded, "Girls, really, you shouldn't fight."

"We're not fighting, Auntie," Juliet reassured her. To her sisters, she asked, "Have any of you talked to Father about the document?"

Portia sat on the arm of the settee. "No. He's still off in Europe with what's-her-face."

Rissa began to pace. "Oh, don't get me started on that tickle-brained baggage. Let me tell you—"

Juliet suppressed a giggle at Rissa's use of a Shakespearean insult.

"I hate this," Miranda blurted out. "Families shouldn't be like this."

Juliet didn't know what a normal family was supposed to feel like.

Aunt Winnie put an arm around Miranda. "Don't upset yourself, dear. It's not good for you."

Rissa whirled around to face her sisters. "I sometimes feel like I'm stuck in a bad soap opera."

A smiled tugged at Juliet's mouth. Leave it to the artsy playwright, Rissa, to put things in perspective. The situation *was* a bit melodramatic. But for now it was their reality. "We have each other, don't we?"

"Of course we do," Bianca agreed. The others all nodded.

"Then we stick together," Juliet stated firmly. "If you need to pursue looking for Mother, then we all do."

Bianca gave her a grateful smile. "I want to start with the night Mother died. We all heard the raised voices. I want to know what that was about."

Tightness pulled at Juliet's chest. She'd been only a baby that night. She had no memories of her mother at all, not even the sound of her raised voice, to cling to.

Rissa snorted. "Only Father can tell us, and you know he wouldn't, even if he were home."

"What about Grandfather? Would he know anything?" Juliet asked.

Portia shrugged. "I'll ask him. But he's not doing so well these days."

Portia and their grandfather had always had a good relationship. Juliet had even less of a relationship with her grandfather than she did with her father. Not that long ago, at Aunt Winnie's sixtieth birthday party, Grandfather had nearly attacked Juliet because he'd thought she was her mother. This only supported Juliet's theory that the Blanchard men kept Juliet at an emotional distance because she looked too much like her mother.

Judging from the few pictures Aunt Winnie had been able to tuck away of Trudy Blanchard, Juliet could easily have passed as Trudy's sister. They both had the same long, platinum-blond hair and green eyes.

"Well, I can snoop around the company and Father's office to see if I can find out anything," Juliet offered.

"No!" Portia exclaimed.

"You shouldn't," Miranda said, her eyes wide with worry.

Bianca shook her head. "You concentrate on your new job. Let us do the investigating."

Not telling them what to do with their patronizing and overbearing protectiveness took every ounce of self-control Juliet possessed. They were her sisters and they loved her, this she knew, but sometimes...being the baby stank.

"Whoa. Wait a sec." Juliet stood. "You all just agreed that we're in this together. And I'll do my part. Looking in the factory for some answers makes sense."

Bianca rose, as well. "Honey, please. None of us want to see you do anything to jeopardize your new career."

A career Juliet didn't want. She bit her tongue. This job was an opportunity to prove herself to them. But that didn't mean she would become a pliable puppet. "I'll do what I'm going to do."

"We all just worry about you, Juliet. You're our baby sister. We want you to make something of your life," Rissa explained.

Juliet's teeth clenched at the reminder of exactly how they all saw her—as some wayward child without any prospects. Granted, she hadn't applied herself in high school and barely managed to squeak by. Her first few quarters of college weren't much better.

But she'd decided it was time to make evident her capabilities. She'd applied herself to school after a few romps around Europe. Now she'd graduated with a degree and a job prospect that they and their father approved of. She'd show them.

Aunt Winnie stood. "Enough of this for now, girls. Let's have a nice dinner and enjoy the rest of our time together before the twins and Bianca have to leave."

Miranda rose and adjusted the skirt of the matronly dress she wore. "You're right, Aunt Winnie. We're being boorish with all this bickering. I want to hear about Rissa's new play."

Taking the cue, the girls filed out of the parlor. Juliet and Bianca were the last to leave the room.

"Juliet, promise me you won't do anything that would get you in trouble with Father," Bianca said.

"I'll only get in trouble if I get caught," Juliet quipped, reciting her childhood motto.

Growing up under the oppressive decorum of the Blanchard name, Juliet had tried to conform, but there were times when she had to let her true impulsive nature loose. Which only distressed her siblings. All but Delia, who was even more reckless in some ways.

At Bianca's pained grimace, Juliet hugged her. "Don't worry, sis. I'll make you proud. Believe me, I don't want to do anything that would give Father a reason to fire me. I know this opportunity will be good for me."

"I think it says a lot that he's giving you the marketing director position. Father was very pleased with your grades last term."

For the first time in Juliet's life, her father seemed proud of her. She'd worked hard to earn those As. And it was gratifying to know he'd noticed. "It stinks that he won't be there to greet me on my first day at the company."

Bianca sighed. "I know. I'm sorry for that."

Juliet made a dismissing noise. "Not your fault."

"But still…"

Juliet wished she could ease her sister's grim expression. Dear Bianca took it upon herself to make sure Juliet was okay. Just as she had Juliet's whole life.

Juliet gave her older sister another quick hug. "I love you, sis. And I thank God for you every day."

"And I, you," Bianca responded with a smile.

As they crossed the hall toward the dining room, Juliet linked her arm through Bianca's. "So, tell me how you and Leo are doing."

Bianca blushed. "Well. Very well."

Happy for her sister, Juliet let her mind wander to a certain man whom she'd had a hard time forgetting. She wondered where Brandon De Witte was. And with whom.

She chided herself for such thoughts. Brandon didn't matter. Couldn't matter. He was a pleasant memory that would eventually fade.

Juliet had more important concerns, such as her first day at the company looming ahead and finding some way to help in the search for their mother.

# THREE

Monday morning arrived, with an overcast sky left behind by the weekend's storm. A chill hung in the manor house as Juliet made her way downstairs for some coffee before heading to Blanchard Fabrics. She wished Bianca and the twins hadn't had to leave yesterday not long after church. Miranda had spent most of the afternoon in her rooms, which left Juliet rambling around with nothing to do. So she'd spent most of the day rummaging through their father's home office. Unfortunately, she didn't find anything of interest.

To help keep her nervousness about her new job from overwhelming her, she contemplated how she'd grab a moment when she could sneak into her father's office and see what she could learn that might help her sisters in their quest to locate their mother.

"Miss Juliet," Marco said as Juliet entered the kitchen. As always, his white uniform was pressed and clean. His dark Latin eyes twinkled with good humor. "Fresh coffee and some pecan sticky buns."

"Yum," Juliet replied with a grin and accepted the travel mug of hot liquid and a wrapped pastry. "Thank you. What a wonderful way to start the day."

"I'll be making apple crisp for tonight." Marco hurried forward to help her slip on the heavy parka over her pink chenille sweater and long, flowered, ruffled skirt.

"I'm going to gain weight living here," Juliet complained with a smile and wave goodbye.

The drive to Blanchard Fabrics took all of ten minutes. In good weather, Juliet vowed she'd walk, if only to work off the sweets that she couldn't resist. She parked in her father's parking space since he wouldn't be in. The big, imposing redbrick building with its many smokestacks loomed against the gray clouds.

Juliet entered the building through the glass double doors and shivered at the blast of warm air from the overhead heaters. She slipped off her parka and approached the reception desk.

The unfamiliar woman sitting behind the counter smiled politely at her. "Can I help you?"

Leaning on the counter, Juliet smiled back. "Juliet Blanchard. I'm supposed to report to Barbara Sanchez."

"Ah, yes." She nodded. "Ms. Sanchez is expecting you. Her office is on the fourth floor, just down the hall from your father's."

"Great, thanks," Juliet replied and hurried to catch the elevator.

The fourth floor looked nothing like what Juliet remembered from her childhood. Her sister Miranda had mentioned that their father had remodeled the offices a few years ago. The linoleum and old-fashioned cubicle dividers that once made up the office spaces had been replaced with lush, sage-green carpet and real wood office walls.

As Juliet proceeded down the hall, she passed a conference room with a long table surrounded by over a dozen padded leather chairs.

She paused at her father's office. The door was closed. She tried the handle. Locked.

"Juliet?"

Her heart jumping in her chest, Juliet spun around to face the woman who'd come up behind her. Her father's longtime executive assistant, Barbara Sanchez, regarded her with interest. Barbara was tall and slightly overweight, but she dressed in very upscale corporate attire that accentuated her olive skin and shiny black hair. "Barbara, hi. I assume Father gave you the lowdown on what I'm to be doing here."

"Yes, of course," Barbara replied, giving her a quizzical look. "Did you need something in your father's office?"

Juliet mentally scrambled. She did want in there to poke around and see if she could find anything about her mother, but telling Barbara as much probably wasn't a good idea. Barbara was very loyal to Juliet's father. Probably not someone she could rely on as an ally. "I was thinking maybe his itinerary would be on his desk. Do you know when my father is expected back from Europe?"

Barbara's nostrils flared slightly as displeasure entered her ebony eyes. "No. Your father has not kept a very reliable schedule ever since he took up with that woman."

Interesting. So, Barbara didn't think very highly of Juliet's father's newest girlfriend. Juliet wondered if she'd liked *any* of the women who'd come parading through Ronald's life. "I've only met Alannah twice. She seems a bit…flamboyant for Father."

Barbara's lip curled. "More like money hungry."

Great. One more *problem* for her and her sisters to face. "Should we be worried?"

Barbara waved off the concern. "Oh, please. Ronald's just indulging in a little midlife philandering. He'll come around eventually."

"I'll pray that he does," Juliet murmured, hating that her father was so cavalier with his soul. Didn't he realize the mess he was making of everyone's lives with his womanizing? She wondered if Barbara had a *personal* interest in Ronald Blanchard. And Juliet didn't know what to feel about that.

"Come, let me show you where you'll be working," Barbara said and headed down the hall away from Ronald's office.

Juliet followed along, peering in the other offices as she went. She waved when she recognized several of the long-term employees, mainly the ones in the sales department who had attended various functions over the years at Blanchard Manor.

Barbara stopped at a small office with a tiny, square window up high on the plain beige wall. There was a bare desk, a filing cabinet and a couple of shelves.

"Here you go," Barbara announced.

Juliet frowned. She'd have thought the marketing director's office would at least have a view. She stepped inside and put her purse on the desk. "So, when do I meet the staff and find out what we're currently working on?"

"There will be a staff meeting in ten minutes in the conference room. You'll see everyone then." Barbara gave her an indulgent smile. "Take a few minutes to settle in and look around. I'm sure you're anxious to meet your new boss."

Juliet cocked her head to one side. "I won't be reporting directly to my father?"

"Oh, mercy, no. Your father has little to do with

the day-to-day operations anymore. Especially now that he's off gallivanting with that woman."

"Right." Of course there'd be someone else in charge while her father was away. Leo used to be that person, but now that he was gone…Juliet could only hope she'd get along with the person in charge.

"We'll see you in ten minutes," Barbara stated before disappearing out of the office.

Juliet sat at the desk and looked through the drawers. All the basic supplies. Bored, she drummed her fingers on the wooden top. She wished she had paper and a charcoal pencil so she could sketch. Instead she tried to think of ways she could get into her father's office.

Finally, she left her little space with pen and spiral notebook in hand and headed down the hall to the conference room she'd passed on her way to her office. A few early birds were already seated at the table.

Juliet joined them, introduced herself and asked what department each worked in and for how long. Soon others began to file in and the room filled. The seats were all taken and a few people stood along the walls.

Barbara strode to the front of the room. She welcomed everyone. "We have another new employee joining us today. Juliet, would you please stand?"

Aware of everyone's attention, Juliet rose with

a smile. She wondered who else had recently joined the company.

"This is Juliet Blanchard, Ronald's youngest daughter. She is coming on board in the marketing department. She recently graduated from Vermont State University with a degree in design and a minor in marketing. Please, welcome Juliet."

Finding it odd that Barbara didn't state exactly what Juliet's position in the marketing department would be, she fought back a wave of unease. The clapping and voices raised in greeting distracted her from Barbara's omission.

As Juliet sank back into her seat, the honey-blond-haired woman seated beside her leaned over to whisper her welcome.

"Hi, I'm Annie Miller. I was in the same high school class as the twins."

Juliet shook the woman's hand and whispered back, "Nice to meet you."

"How are your sisters?"

"Good. Rissa has a play being produced on Broadway and Portia's arts store is thriving. They were—"

"Ladies, do you mind?"

Juliet started at the deep, familiar voice. Her gaze flew to the man who moved to stand at the head of the long conference table.

She blinked, sure she was seeing things.

But no, what she saw was real.

Brandon De Witte, looking roguishly handsome in a traditional navy business suit, was staring at her with an amused glint in his brown eyes and a secret smile on his full lips.

Stunned, all Juliet could do was stare back. Apparently her hope of seeing him again one day had come true.

But at Blanchard Fabrics?

After she'd kissed him? Definitely a shocker, not to mention the potential for embarrassment.

A lump of sinking dread hit the bottom of her stomach as something even more threatening came into focus. Brandon De Witte's only interest was in companies that were struggling.

Was her father's company in trouble?

Brandon watched the color drain from Juliet's lovely face and wondered for a second if she'd pass out from shock.

He could only imagine her reaction if she knew that ruining her father's company was his plan. An eye for an eye and all that.

He shifted his attention to the rest of the group, said what he needed to say and then dismissed them.

"Would the marketing team please stay for a moment?" he asked as the staff began to leave.

Juliet stayed in her chair, her big green eyes watching him closely. When the four marketing department members were seated around the table, he brought out the new marketing campaign that Ronald Blanchard had approved before going off to Europe.

"Wait a second." Juliet held up a staying hand. "Where did you get this?"

"Your father," he replied smoothly and then continued on. The campaign was simple, yet he knew it would be effective in propelling Blanchard Fabrics forward in the changing marketplace and would help raise the company's lagging profit margin.

Brandon had come up with the idea as a way to leverage a position in the company. But he and his uncle planned to take over the company before the campaign was implemented. Brandon had heard through the business grapevine that Ronald Blanchard's right-hand man was leaving the company, as well as the marketing director. He'd quickly abandoned his earlier plan of ingratiating himself with the Blanchards through Juliet. Instead he'd opted for the better way to bring down the company by infiltrating the inner workings.

Ronald had been impressed with his credentials and quickly hired Brandon to step into the marketing director's position. And now that Ronald was out for a while, he'd basically left Brandon in charge. How much easier could taking down the Blanchards be?

He glanced at Juliet, who stared at him with suspicion. When he heard that Juliet would be working under his direction and that her father wanted him to basically teach her everything he knew, he'd vowed not to let the unexpected twist interfere with his plan.

He'd had a hard time not thinking about her after their evening together. Who knows what had possessed him to kiss her? That hadn't been planned. Nor had enjoying Juliet's company been anticipated. She hadn't been as spoiled or as superficial as he'd been led to believe.

But, he reminded himself, she was a Blanchard. And the Blanchards would pay for the things they'd done to his family.

Returning his attention to the marketing plan, he assigned different tasks to the members and then dismissed them. All except Juliet. Time for damage control.

When they were alone, she faced him. "What gives?"

"Excuse me?"

"What are you doing here?"

Brandon pulled up a chair and leaned back with his fingers steepled over his chest. "I'm working here, or weren't you paying attention?"

She narrowed her gaze to icy slits. "Why? Is the company in trouble?"

"Now, Juliet, why would you ask such a question?"

"Don't get smart with me, Mr. Corporate Raider.

You said yourself that you find companies in trouble and buy them or revitalize them. So *is* the company in trouble?"

Boy, she was sassy. He rather liked that about her. "Not in any trouble that can't be fixed. Profits are down, but we'll get them to where they should be." A big, fat, red zero.

"When did my father hire you? Before or after?"

Knowing full well what she meant, he pretended otherwise. "Before or after what?"

She pressed her lush mouth into a severe line and went in a different direction. "So you're taking over for Leo?"

He shook his head. "Just until your father returns. Then I'll concentrate on what I was hired to do."

"Which is?" she ground out.

"I'm the new marketing director."

*"What?"* She jumped to her feet.

"Are you going to have a problem working for me?" he asked, keeping his voice mild.

"*I'm* supposed to be the director," she huffed, her fair complexion turning red.

That was news to him. Hmm. This could work to his advantage. "Apparently your father missed that memo." He really shouldn't bait her, but he was enjoying the passion and fire darkening the color in her eyes to a deep forest green.

She made a low, growling noise in her throat.

"We'll see." She huffed from the room, skirt swirling about her booted ankles and her shiny, long hair bouncing down her back.

She really was even lovelier than he remembered. He tapped a finger to his lips. Better to keep in mind there was no room for romance in revenge.

Shoulders ridged and hands clenched at her sides, Juliet slammed into Barbara's office.

The older woman looked up with a startled gaze. "Juliet, is something wrong?"

"Yes, something is wrong. That…that man is in *my* job."

Barbara's eyebrows pulled together in puzzlement. "I don't understand."

"Neither do I," Juliet muttered and slumped into the chair opposite Barbara. "I need to talk to my father."

"That's impossible."

"Nothing's impossible. You must have a way to reach him." It occurred to her that Bianca would have a number. But Juliet would rather not drag her sisters into this until she'd talked with her father. Her siblings would never stop babying her if she called them for help every time she was in trouble. There had to be a rational explanation for why Brandon De Witte was here.

"The number I have is for emergencies only," Barbara stated.

Juliet sat up straight. "This *is* an emergency! *I'm* supposed to be the marketing director."

Barbara shook her head. "I don't think a mix-up in your job position would constitute an emergency in your father's eyes."

"Maybe not, but *I* don't have a problem with interrupting his vacation." Juliet raised her eyebrows in challenge. "Do *you?*"

A slow smile spread across Barbara's face. "No, actually, I don't." She reached into a drawer and drew out a card. "Here." She handed the number to Juliet.

Fingering the card, Juliet said, "I'd like the keys to my father's office. I'm sure what I have to say should be done in complete privacy."

Barbara tilted her head. "And you can't use your new office because…"

Juliet scrambled for an answer. "I'll feel closer to him if I'm sitting in his chair." The excuse sounded lame, but it was the best she could come up with. Hopefully it was good enough for her father's assistant.

After a moment's hesitation, Barbara handed over a set of keys. "The long silver one opens the door."

"Thank you," Juliet said and palmed the keys, making a mental note to make copies before giving them back.

She hurried down the hall to her father's office, unlocked the door and stepped into the dark interior. The faint scent of her father's spicy after-shave lingered in the air. Leaning back against the door, she fought the pang of yearning that over-whelmed her at odd moments.

As a child, she'd loved to curl up in her father's bed and breathe deeply of his masculine scent clinging to the pillows. It made her feel close to him. Then one day he'd caught her and banned her from his room forever.

Hurt, she'd left, but she hadn't gone very far when she heard her father's sobs. She'd gone back and peeked inside. Seeing her strong, formidable father kneeling beside the bed crying had hurt worse than anything could. Because she knew that she reminded him too much of his late wife. Juliet had never told anyone.

Pushing away the bleak memory, she flipped on the overhead light. The room was so close to a replica of her father's study at the manor that for a moment Juliet was speechless.

Giving herself a mental shake, she went to the phone. Sinking into her father's high-backed leather chair, she dialed the international number that Barbara had given to her. On the third ring, a woman answered in a sultry, sleepy voice. "Hello?"

Certain that the woman on the other end of the line was Alannah, Juliet said, "This is Juliet. I need to speak to my father."

Impatient, Juliet listened to the shuffling sound

of the phone being handed over and the muted voices of Alannah and Ronald; then he came on the line. "Juliet?"

"Hello, Father. Sorry to bother you but I have a problem here."

"Did something happen to one of your sisters?" he asked, his voice harsh with concern.

She closed her eyes against the disappointment and hurt at his apparent lack of concern for her. "No. Everyone is fine."

"Then why are you calling?"

Bolstering her courage to confront her father, she said, "I came to work this morning as planned, only there seems to be a mix-up. There's this man claiming to be the marketing director. But you told me I would have that position if I came to work here."

"*That's* why you're calling?"

Juliet gritted her teeth against the disdain lacing his words. "Yes. This is not what we agreed upon."

"Juliet, you're young, untried and inexperienced. The more I thought about it, the more I realized that bringing you in as the director was not a good move. When De Witte approached me with his ideas, I knew I had to hire him."

She let out an angry, exasperated noise. "You could have told me."

"I forgot," he said rather irritably.

Of course he had. Hurt and bitterness threatened to choke her. She always came last in his priorities.

She had hoped coming to work for him as he'd wanted would finally make a difference, that he'd finally come to respect her. To see her as a capable woman worthy of his affection.

"Juliet?"

"I'm here," she forced out.

"When I return we'll discuss this further. Until then, use this opportunity to learn from De Witte. And don't call me again unless it's a life-or-death situation." He hung up.

Juliet stared at the phone handset, her jaw tight. Did strangling her new boss count as a life-or-death situation?

# FOUR

"**B**randon? Why are you in my father's office?"

Brandon paused, checked the grimace that tightened his jaw and then slowly straightened to face Juliet. She'd regarded him with wary suspicion for the past week and today was no different.

She stood in the open doorway of her father's office looking like springtime in winter and out of place. Her tiered skirt and lacy top, which hugged her curvy figure to perfection, were better suited for the artsy world of fashion design than for a professional place of business.

He'd found himself wondering over the last week why in the world she was working for Blanchard Fabrics rather than in the world of fashion. She had real talent as a designer; he hadn't lied about that.

"Good morning to you, too." He noticed the set of keys she held in one hand. He hadn't heard her unlock the door. He'd been too focused on looking through Ronald's desk, searching for his personal financial records.

"I asked you a question," she said and stepped closer.

He picked up a file folder. "We have the Reynolds people coming in a few days. We need to be prepared."

She tilted her head to one side. "Why didn't you ask Barbara to find whatever you needed?"

He smiled. "Who do you think let me in?"

Her lips compressed into a tight, disapproving line. She'd made little effort to disguise her animosity toward him. Because he was in her job or because she'd kissed a man who was now her boss?

She hadn't broached the subject of their kiss since that first day. Now might be a good time to distract her from asking any more questions about why he was rifling through her father's desk. He had no qualms about manipulating this beautiful woman to further his plans to bring her family to their knees. After what they'd done to his family, he'd do anything to that end.

Maybe he should capitalize on their mutual attraction. "Do you have a moment so we could talk?"

Her shoulder rose in a noncommittal shrug. "I suppose."

He moved to close the door and then sat in one of the two leather captain's chairs that faced the desk. He motioned for her to take the other chair. "Juliet."

Slowly, she sat. Her white-blond hair slid across the back of the chair in stark contrast to the dark leather. "Okay, boss man. Talk."

His mouth quirked with genuine amusement. He liked that she didn't bother to put up a front with people. She said what was on her mind. "That bugs you, doesn't it? That your father put me in charge?"

She looked away but the expression on her face said everything. Resentment, anger and a bit of embarrassment.

Taking her hand, he leaned forward. Her wide-eyed gaze swung back to him. Lightly, he traced the lines of her palm. Her hand was soft and fragile and fit perfectly in his. Too perfectly.

It wasn't too hard to see how she felt about his taking her job. Clearly, she was hurt and upset. He recalled the question she'd asked him that first day. He would answer it honestly now after she'd lost the job she'd been promised. She deserved that at least. "Your first day here, you asked me if I knew when we'd had dinner if I was going to take this job. No, I didn't know. Juliet, I didn't ask to be your boss or deliberately take your position. I had no idea until after I came on board that you would be coming to work here. I thought you'd be off starting your career in the fashion world."

She blinked, surprise clear in the depths of her

eyes. "So you weren't using me to get to my father?"

The accuracy of the question bit into his conscience. That had been the original plan. But he'd taken the more direct route to his revenge and hadn't expected to see the lovely Juliet again.

He squelched any sentiment that even resembled guilt, unwilling to waver in his resolve. "Juliet, you are a very attractive and interesting woman, one who should be off designing clothes for the rich and famous. Why aren't you?"

She sighed. "My family thinks my being here is for the best."

"But it's not what *you* want, so what are you doing working here?"

He really was curious about her, about what made her tick. She was a fascinating mixture of strength and vulnerability. If she wasn't from his sworn enemy's family, he'd— No. He refused to even contemplate that scenario. She was a Blanchard. He had to remember that.

"I just am," she replied. "My father thinks I'll learn a lot from you."

Brandon raised an eyebrow. "That's flattering. I'll be more than happy to teach you anything you want to know."

A calculating look entered her eyes. "I'll take you up on that. I want to be able to impress my father when he returns from his trip."

Obviously Juliet was angling for his job. He mentally snorted. There wouldn't be a job after he was done destroying Blanchard Fabrics. But he'd make sure she learned something from him.

And not because he felt any guilt for his plans or the hurt she'd inevitably feel.

He'd teach her the ropes because becoming her mentor in the workplace could only further his agenda and hopefully gain him access to the rest of the cold and corrupt family.

By the next week, Juliet was feeling more confident and sure of herself in the workplace. Brandon had been true to his word and had tirelessly answered all of her questions, taught her more about the marketing field than she'd learned in her years of college and had respected her enough to let her take the reins occasionally.

His genius was amazing and the way he handled the clients left her speechless. No wonder her father had hired him. Everyone in the company was excited and a renewed sense of fire swept through the employees.

There were only two downsides to working with Brandon.

One, she'd searched her father's office, both at work and at home in hopes of finding some clue about her mother, but had come up empty. A couple of times, she found Brandon in her father's office at the factory going through files and looking at financial statements. But she shrugged off any suspicions when he explained he was only doing his job.

The other downside in working so closely with Brandon was the yearning he stirred in her heart for a more personal relationship with him. Though he was careful to keep his distance both physically and emotionally.

Not enough space to make her think he was not interested in her at all, because he clearly was if she read the occasional look she caught in his brown eyes correctly. But still, she wondered if that one evening they'd spent together had made any impact on him.

And he hadn't asked to kiss her again. Boy, she wished he would.

She admired his work ethic and appreciated his confidence in her. She liked watching him in action when he was creating or presenting or even when he was quietly working at his desk.

But she especially enjoyed watching him up close and personal, like now, as they worked together on the marketing campaign. They sat in the conference room brainstorming ideas for the storyboard that would eventually be a televised ad.

Brandon had insisted they could come up with the ad in-house rather than outsourcing the work to an advertising company. A commercial production company was scheduled to start producing the ad on Monday. So it was important that they finish the project in the next few days.

It was past quitting time, and most of the office staff had long since gone home. Through the conference room window the dusky evening sky was giving way to full-fledged night. Juliet rolled her stiff shoulders. She'd been sketching ideas for hours. Her hand was beginning to cramp and her stomach reminded her that dinner with her sisters was waiting at home for her.

"I was wondering what you have planned for tonight," she blurted out to Brandon.

He paused in the act of writing copy for the ad. "Tonight?"

She put down her charcoal pencil. "I was hoping you'd come to dinner with me."

He sat back and studied her. "Juliet, are you asking me for a date?"

She frowned. "No. I mean, yes. I mean, I'd like to take you home with me."

He arched both brows. She realized how that sounded and quickly scrambled to explain. "My sisters are all home tonight, that is, except Delia, and I thought, if you don't have other plans, that you might want to come to dinner at the manor. I mean, it's late, and I really don't want to miss the time with my family. My sisters' visits are often short and sporadic."

A slow smile spread across his handsome face. "That would be great."

"Great," Juliet repeated, squelching the silly desire to dance around the room in giddy anticipation.

He followed her to the Blanchard Estate in his own SUV. She kept glancing back in the rearview mirror to make sure he was still there. She'd dated casually through college but had never brought a man home to meet her family. But since Father already approved of Brandon, she wanted to see what her sisters thought of him.

Just in case she ever got up the nerve to see where a relationship with him could go.

Brandon couldn't believe his luck. He was actually setting foot inside the Blanchard estate. The cold and imposing house did little to welcome him. All the riches in the place were bought with his family's blood. Deep-seated anger stirred but he was careful to keep it under control. He couldn't blow this opportunity to ingratiate himself into the clan's fold.

Juliet had talked nonstop since they'd arrived. Her nervousness was endearing. He had the distinct impression that he was being brought home for approval from the family. He supposed he should be intimidated to be meeting four of the five other Blanchard sisters, but instead, he felt a steely determination to ferret out the family's weaknesses any way he could.

Juliet led him to the parlor where the women had gathered. He blinked as he took in the Blanchard ladies. Four stunningly beautiful, dark-haired, dark-eyed women assessed him with interest and intelligence.

An older woman with fading red hair stared at him with something akin to shock in her hazel eyes. Juliet noticed the older woman's distress and hurried over to her.

"Auntie, are you all right?" she asked as she helped her aunt to sit on the small couch.

"I'm fine, dear. I grew a little light-headed for a moment."

Juliet exchanged a concerned glance with each sister as they all gathered around their aunt, completely ignoring Brandon. One of the petite twins rushed out of the room and returned with a glass of water.

Brandon felt like an intruder watching the display of affection among the women as they hovered about their aunt. One of the women rose and strode toward him. She had an air of authority in her bearing and by the chic power suit she wore, he guessed she was the lawyer.

"Hello. You must be Brandon." She stuck out her hand. "I'm Bianca. Juliet has told us so much about you."

He shook her hand, noting the firm, solid pressure, so unlike Juliet's more delicate handshake. This woman would eat him alive if she knew what he was planning. He smiled. "It's nice to meet you. I hope this isn't a bad time for a visit."

Their aunt waved the girls away and stood. "Nonsense. This is a wonderful time." She moved forward and the girls stayed close to her side. "We are happy to have Juliet's young man in our house."

Unexpectedly, warm pleasure spread through him at being referred to as Juliet's young man. It only felt good because being romantically linked to Juliet would further his plan, not because of any real feelings he might harbor for her.

Juliet's cheeks reddened. "Auntie, this is Brandon. Brandon, my Aunt Winnie."

Brandon shook the older woman's hand. "My pleasure."

Juliet introduced him to the other Blanchard women. Soon they moved to the dining room. Brandon sat between Juliet and Rissa, the playwright.

At first he listened to the women's discussions with an ear toward learning something to use against them. But soon he found himself enjoying the lively ladies and becoming increasingly charmed with Juliet. She challenged her sisters with her quick wit and kept him included in the conversation.

The love and affection so evident in the way the women related to one another was something Brandon had never experienced. He was an only child and had been raised by his unmarried uncle, who'd drilled into Brandon at a young age a hatred for all things Blanchard.

But these kindhearted women were nothing like the stories of the cold, corrupt clan that had been instilled in him his whole life. In light of this, his uncle's hatred for the Blanchards seemed out of proportion with the wrong done his family. Was there more to his uncle's feelings than what he'd told Brandon?

Confusion and doubts gnawed at him, especially every time he met Winnie's hazel eyes. She watched him with a dreamy, sad look that left him unsettled.

"I apologize for staring," Winnie said at one point. "Were you at the Winter Festival last month?"

He shook his head. "No."

Winnie's eyebrows drew slightly together. "Odd. I thought perhaps I'd seen you there. You look so much like a man I once knew. It's uncanny."

He knew his looks favored his Uncle Tate and it occurred to him that his uncle and Juliet's aunt were of the same age. Could the man Winnie mentioned be Brandon's uncle? If so, then Brandon would need to be very careful.

Reminding himself to stay focused on his goal

of bringing down this family, Brandon managed to slip away from the ladies on the pretext of using the phone in their father's study when they all retired back to the parlor. He hoped to find some incriminating evidence that could help him in his plan to ruin Blanchard Fabrics. The study closely resembled Ronald's office at the factory. After a quick search through the drawers, Brandon decided he needed to find Ronald's private quarters. Perhaps there, Brandon would come across something useful.

He slipped up the stairs, having already ascertained from Juliet through casual conversation the location of her father's rooms. As Brandon reached the landing where the second-floor stairs and the third-floor stairs met he was stopped by a disheveled man descending the stairs from the third floor.

"You!" the man shouted and pointed one rickety finger at Brandon.

"I'm sorry?"

The man stumbled down a few more stairs. "I told you, Connolly, to go away and never come back. What are you doing here? You can't have my daughter!"

Brandon drew back as if the old man had slapped him. Why would he call him by his mother's maiden name? What was the old man talking about? This had to be the elder Blanchard, Howard. Brandon had heard the man was not well. He certainly didn't look well. His nightclothes were askew and his gray hair stuck out in all directions.

The old man swayed slightly and Brandon rushed up the stairs to grab him to keep him from falling.

Howard flinched, his eyes wild with sudden fear. "No! No, don't hurt me!"

"I wouldn't hurt you," Brandon said in as reassuring a voice as he could. His heart pounded in his chest. Why would this man think he was here to hurt him?

"Howard! Howard, what are you doing?" A woman wearing a traditional white nurse's uniform came hurrying up the stairs carrying a tray with a cup, saucer and a teapot. She reached their side, shoved the tray into Brandon's hands, then took Howard by the arm and led him back up the stairs to the third floor.

Following with the tray, Brandon realized his hands were shaking. Obviously there *was* more to the Connolly-Blanchard feud than Uncle Tate had told him. But what?

Brandon resolved to find out.

When the nurse was done securing Howard in his bed, she came hurrying toward him. "Sorry about that. I only left him for a moment to bring him his nightly tea. It's the housekeeper's night off. My name is Peg. I'm Howard's full-time nurse. Are you lost?" the woman asked as she took the tray from Brandon.

Brandon ran a hand through his hair and gave a slight shrug. "I must have taken a wrong turn. I didn't mean to upset him. I think he thought I was someone else."

Peg shrugged slightly. "He's constantly doing that. Just a couple of months ago he attacked poor Juliet because he thought she was her mother. He obviously wasn't fond of Trudy."

Brandon's insides clenched with a fierce, unexpected surge of protectiveness toward Juliet. "She wasn't hurt, was she?"

"No, no. Just upset. Here I am, telling tales. Shame on me. You must be one of the girls' guest. I'm sure they'll be wondering where you are." She balanced the tray on one hand and shooed Brandon out the door with the other.

Brandon couldn't bring himself to reenter the Blanchard women's world. He wanted answers to the questions that had arisen this evening so as to be more fully equipped to bring down the Blanchards. He dismissed the very idea that somehow he was wrong in wanting to destroy the family.

Nothing could change the fact that the Blanchards were ultimately responsible for Brandon's parents' death.

Every time he thought of his parents, the pain of loss sharpened his need for revenge. But doubts tried to dull the edges. He had to get out of here.

He raced down the stairs to leave and stopped short when he saw Juliet.

"Brandon?" She approached, concern etched in her beautiful face.

That protectiveness surged again, choking in its intensity. He thought of her ill grandfather attacking her and he wanted to wrap his arms around her and protect her. "I have to leave," he said, his voice coming out harsh. He winced at the way Juliet drew back. He softened his tone. "Something's come up. I'm sorry."

"Something with the company?" Her voice rose slightly.

He shook his head. "No. Personal business." That was true enough.

He walked toward the coatrack. Juliet followed. As he put on his overcoat, Juliet grabbed a puffy down jacket from the rack. She zipped it up and secured the hood. The fur-lined hood rimmed her lovely face. She looked adorable and vulnerable in the jacket.

"You don't have to walk me out," he said.

She grinned. "I know. I want to. Can you stay long enough for me to show you the grounds?"

His need to rush off slowly evaporated as he stared into Juliet's beautiful eyes. When it was just the two of them, it was too easy to let her become the center of his attention. He nodded.

She steered him away from the front door and took him out the back.

Glad for the cold night air hitting his face and slapping his thoughts back into place, he asked, "Where are we going?"

"We'll walk through the garden around to the front," she said and looped her arm through his.

The intimacy of the gesture made his insides clench. The pressure of her arm, even through the layers of heavy clothing, brought a pleasant rush to his senses.

The view off the cliffs was magnificent with the moon's light casting long arms of light over the churning water. The scent of earth, sea and foliage brought a strange sense of peace to him.

Juliet talked about the garden, pointing to the gazebo, and went on about the whales in the spring. She stopped and directed his gaze upward to the stone mansion. "That's my room there. The turret room with the balcony."

"Ah. Fitting for a beautiful rose named Juliet," he murmured.

She gazed up at him with such a beguiling wistfulness that his heart contracted painfully in his chest. His gaze dropped to her mouth. Her lips parted in invitation.

"'Tempt not a desperate man,'" he said, quoting the old Bard, holding himself still, willing himself not to give in to the yearning to kiss his sweet Juliet again. She was, after all, the enemy.

She gave a soft laugh and sadness crept into her

eyes. "Supposedly, my mother quoted Shakespeare all the time. She died not long after I was born."

"I'd heard that." He sometimes wondered if having no memory of his parents wouldn't be preferable to the memories that haunted him. "I didn't mean to make you sad."

"It's okay. I like that you know Shakespeare. Most guys don't." To his relief, she started walking again.

At his car, he said, "Good night, Juliet."

Even though he should be running as fast as he could from her, he was reluctant to leave her.

"Drive carefully," she said but made no move to return to the house.

He tucked a stray strand of hair into the hood. "I will."

It was a mistake to touch her. His hand slid around the curve of her ear and to the pulse point on her graceful neck. Drawn to her in a way he'd never been before with any other woman, he leaned toward her and she met his lips. The kiss was chaste, gentle and achingly tender and left him off-kilter as they parted.

"I'll see you tomorrow," he murmured.

She nodded and fled, as if she, too, had been deeply affected by the kiss. More so than the kiss they'd shared before. That kiss had been of need and passion, this was of caring and…

He climbed in his car and wished he could pray

for strength. But praying wasn't his style; that had been his father's way, and look where he'd ended up. In the grave.

Besides, Brandon doubted God would help a man bent on revenge. In fact, God would probably find it funny that Brandon was falling for the enemy.

# FIVE

Juliet lay in her bed with the warm down comforter tucked beneath her chin. The shadows of the trees outside her window danced across the ceiling. Her thoughts turned over and over, reliving that moment when Brandon's mouth had captured hers in a tender caress. A kiss so confusing yet so perfect.

For days on end as they'd worked together, she'd wondered if his kiss would cause the same flutter of pleasure inside her as his first kiss had. Now she knew.

Yes. His kiss, whether passionate or romantic, sweet and laden with romance, affected her, causing pleasure and affection to wrap around her heart.

Whoa! Her heart?

She had no intention of giving her heart to anyone just yet. She had too many things planned. A man in her life would only complicate those plans.

Especially Brandon. They worked together, she was aiming for his job and she had plans for a future in fashion design that didn't include a corporate guru. She wanted her independence.

But still…

She vowed her lips still tingled from the kiss and the gentle caring she'd witnessed in his eyes just before she'd fled to the safety of the house.

Ugh! She was never going to get any sleep with these thoughts rampaging through her brain. She rolled over, taking the comforter with her. A draft of cold air seeped through her flannel pajamas. Frustrated, she rearranged the covers and turned over again, but she couldn't get comfortable.

She glanced at the glowing numbers on the clock sitting on the bedside table. She'd been lying in bed for three hours and sleep was nowhere to be found.

She kicked off the covers, slid into her slippers and robe. Maybe some hot chocolate and one of Marco's sweet concoctions would help. She made her way through the darkened house by the light of the moon glowing through the multipaned windows in the entryway. In the kitchen, she heated up some milk and dumped in a huge serving of milk chocolate. She settled on a bar stool at the large island with her cup of cocoa and a slice of berry pie.

Since she wouldn't let herself think of Brandon, her thoughts swirled around the mystery of her mother. Nothing new had been found in the past two weeks. Bianca had said the forensics on the custodial papers hadn't come back yet. Man, it never took this long on those TV crime shows. The detectives had the whole case solved in under sixty minutes. Too bad real life didn't imitate art that closely.

Searching her father's offices had produced nothing. Her sisters had said they'd already searched his bedroom suite. Juliet had even taken a shot at searching her father's cars, thinking maybe he'd keep something there in a compartment or under the seat. Nothing.

She squelched the twinge of guilt for snooping. Earning her father's respect meant a lot to her, but her sisters' meant more.

Had one of her sisters searched the attic and the basement, as well? Maybe they hadn't. The hour was too late to ask.

Finished with her late-night snack and no closer to feeling sleepy, Juliet contemplated her next move. Should she head down to the dank recesses of the cold, dark basement? Or try the dusty attic?

Considering she was in her pj's, she chose the warmer attic. Careful not to make any noises, she ascended the stairs to the third floor, past her grandfather's suite. No lights showed beneath the big oak doors as she paused to listen. Assured that Grandfather and his nurse, Peg, both were soundly sleeping, she moved farther down the hall to the door that opened to a stairwell leading up to the attic.

The door squeaked slightly, raising the hair on Juliet's nape. She peered into the blackness where only the first few steps were visible. She groped along the wall inside the doorway for the light switch. When she found it, she stepped into the small stairwell, closing the door behind her before flipping the switch.

Light flooded the stairwell and brought welcome relief from the dark. Moving cautiously, placing her feet strategically to miss the squeaky boards that she remembered from her childhood jaunts to the attic, she moved up the stairs. At the top, she reached to pull the string for the overhead light.

The attic was full of old furniture, trunks full of Grandmother Ethel's clothes, a sewing dummy that her aunt used when making the girls' dresses. Shelves full of books lined one wall. A floor-length mirror sat in one corner.

As children, the girls had loved to come to the attic and dress up in their grandmother's old clothes. They would spend hours donning hats and gloves and dresses that dated back to the twenties.

Not sure what she was looking for or where she'd find it, Juliet began with the books on the shelves. Methodically, she pulled each book out, thumbed through the pages and shook it to see if anything lay hidden between the pages. Near the bottom shelf, she found a cardboard box behind a layer of books, a box she'd never seen before.

Moving the books aside, she pulled the box off the shelf. It was a bit heavy as if more books were inside. Gently setting the box on the floor so as not to make a noise that would alert anyone on the floor below of her presence, Juliet sat down beside the box. The top was taped shut. Using her fingernail, she poked and peeled at the aged, yellow tape. When she had broken through the seal on the four sides, she lifted the lid. Dust teased her nose. She muffled a sneeze in the sleeve of her fleece robe.

Just as she suspected, the box was full of books. Textbooks. But whose?

She examined each book. Under one textbook was a class schedule with the name Trudy Blanchard on it. Ah. These had been her mother's books from when she'd gone back to college to become a teacher, right before she'd gotten pregnant with Juliet. Had Trudy not finished college because she was pregnant? Had the thwarted dream of being a teacher contributed to her mother's postpartum depression?

Her mother had once touched these books. Juliet's heart squeezed with sorrow for having never known the woman who'd given her life.

That kicked-in-the-gut feeling Juliet always experienced when she thought about her mother's reasons for abandoning her family and her subsequent "death" hit Juliet hard now. One more heartbreak her birth was responsible for.

She wiped at the tear sliding down her cheek. Self-pity wasn't going to help. Bianca was convinced Trudy was alive. Until they all knew for sure one way or the other, Juliet had to stay focused on helping to bring closure for the sisters she loved.

And for herself.

The last book in the box was her mother's college yearbook. Juliet hugged it to her chest for a moment before opening the cover and searching through the pages for her mother's picture. Finding it, she traced a fingertip over the small square photo. Her pretty green eyes sparkled; her blond hair was cut in a trendy bob. The camera captured her playful smile. A smile Juliet never had the privilege of knowing.

She shut the book and laid it aside so she could refill the box with the textbooks. She'd take the yearbook to her room to show the others in the morning. She was sure they'd want to see another aspect of their mother. After arranging the box just as she'd found it, she picked up the yearbook. Something from between the pages fluttered to the floor.

Blinking, Juliet stared at the photo lying faceup on the ground. Squatting and setting the yearbook down, she gaped at the dog-eared picture of her mother arm in arm with a slightly older man. Her mother's face so happy and carefree, her slim frame clad in a full skirt and pink sweater. The man wore brown slacks and an argyle sweater-vest over a button-down shirt. The couple stood on the steps of the local college's campus entrance and from the way they gazed into each other's eyes, it was clear they had feelings for one another.

Juliet sat down. Her heart hammered in her chest. This had to be from the first time Trudy had attended college. Did her sisters know their mother had had a boyfriend before she'd married their father?

Juliet flipped the picture over with the tip of a fingernail. Her mouth went dry and she began to shake. Written in a neat script that was not her mother's were the words, "Yours always and forever, Arthur."

But it was the date tidily penned in the corner that sucked the breath from her lungs. A day approximately a year prior to Juliet's birth.

The photo was not from Trudy's first years of college but from the second time she'd enrolled.

Which seemed to suggest that her mother had been involved with another man while married to Ronald Blanchard.

Grabbing the photo with shaky hands, Juliet turned it over again to stare at the man in the photo. She blinked several times to clear her mind, because what she was seeing couldn't be true. She slowly rose and moved to stand in front of the floor-length mirror. Her reflection was muted from the aging glass, but what she saw didn't deny what her head didn't want to accept.

She bore an uncanny resemblance to the man in the photo. It was there in the line of his nose and the shape of his jaw, so much like her own.

Her mind jumped and skidded to a conclusion that weakened her knees.

Could this mystery man be her biological father?

She whirled away from the mirror and rushed back to the yearbook. Frantically, she searched every page for more pictures of the man named Arthur, but there were none.

Mind reeling and heart racing, she sank to the floor. Had she always felt like an outsider because she was not Ronald Blanchard's daughter? Was that why Ronald stayed so emotionally detached from his youngest child?

The conclusion made sense.

A silent wail ran through her body, making her shudder as the dream of having Ronald's love cracked.

But how would she tell her sisters she might not be one of them?

She moaned and rocked. "God, how could You let this happen? Why?"

She knew God was in control but she also knew that He allowed humans to make their own choices. Choices that could hurt others.

Staggering to her feet, she left the attic behind

and eased down the third-floor stairs as dawn's first few rays began to filter through the house. She heard someone coming up the stairs from the first floor as she hit the landing on the second floor. Not up to facing anyone at the moment, she ducked in a small alcove that still remained shadowed. Nurse Peg appeared at the top of the stairs carrying a tray with a pot of tea and a cup. Juliet waited until Peg was out of sight on the third floor before hurrying to her own room.

She slid the yearbook under her bed and put the picture in the pocket of her handbag. Before she revealed what she'd discovered to anyone, she had to find out who this Arthur was and exactly what was the relationship between him and her mother.

On autopilot, she showered, dressed and headed downstairs. The kitchen staff was busy preparing the breakfast meal. Her aunt had not come down yet, nor had Miranda. The twins had gone to Portia's last night after dinner and Bianca had caught the last flight to Boston. Juliet went to her aunt's suite and knocked.

"Come in," her aunt called.

Juliet stepped into her aunt's domain. Soft and calming hues of blues and lilacs accented the chairs and antique brass bed. Beautifully framed stills of garden scenes hung along one wall. Lace sheers draped over the window that overlooked the Atlantic Ocean.

"Good morning, dear. Is everything all right?"

Aunt Winnie asked from where she sat in front of her vanity. She had gathered her fading red hair and was twisting it into a knot that she then secured at the back of her nape with a long clip.

Juliet sat on the small couch that faced her aunt. She wanted to open up and tell Winnie what the night had uncovered, but she held back. She wasn't sure sharing her suspicions with anyone in the family would be wise. Her conclusions could be totally wrong and would only hurt her aunt if she realized that Juliet had always felt like an outsider.

"Auntie, I was wondering if you can remember anything unusual about the time when my mother went back to school."

Winnie turned to face her, concern clear in her eyes. "Well, there was tension in your parents' marriage. My brother is not the easiest person to live with. He can be quite demanding and overbearing, as you well know."

She paused, a thoughtful expression suffusing her face. "Your mother wasn't very happy. I think she regretted not finishing college before she married Ronald. Going back to school was a way for her to feel fulfilled."

"But then I came along," Juliet muttered.

Winnie came to sit beside Juliet. Taking her hand, she said, "Now, don't think for a minute your mother wasn't happy about you. Yes, you were unexpected, but Trudy loved all of her children."

A horrible feeling of guilt squirmed in the pit of Juliet's stomach. "Then why did she become so depressed after giving birth to me?"

"I wish I had an answer to that," Winnie replied, her voice sad. "Trudy saw several doctors who assured her that it would take time and medication. Her depression wasn't something she or anyone, save God, could control. And it certainly wasn't your fault."

Juliet wanted to believe that but knowing that her birth caused her mother anguish wasn't something she could forget.

"How did Father take the news when she became pregnant with me?"

Winnie sighed. "He was ecstatic at first. Promised to be a more attentive husband, a better father. And he was, for a time."

"Then what happened?"

"I don't know." Winnie stared off, obviously reflecting on that time. "I've often wondered that myself. A few months after you were born, the tension that had been between them before your birth came back and intensified." Winnie shifted her gaze again to Juliet. "Until…well, until the night she left."

Maybe Ronald had discovered the affair? Juliet tried to keep her confusion and stunned emotions in check.

She stood. "Thank you, Auntie. I'd better go. I'll be late for work."

Winnie gave her a quick hug. "Please try not to let the past upset you, dear. The future is what you make it."

"Thanks, Auntie," Juliet said as she headed to the door.

"Oh, Juliet, I just wanted to tell you that I very much approve of your young man. He was quite charming."

Heat crept up Juliet's neck. "We work together, Auntie. We're not involved."

At least she didn't think they were. But they'd kissed. Twice. She really liked him, enjoyed his company and was learning from him, but taking on a romantic relationship in the middle of trying to figure out the mystery surrounding her birth wasn't a productive idea. She needed to stay focused on her mother and finding out who Arthur was. She wouldn't let her attraction to Brandon interfere.

"If you say so," Winnie stated with a sage nod and a knowing smile.

"You're an incurable romantic, Auntie," Juliet mused with a smile.

As Juliet hurried through the kitchen, Marco held out her travel mug and a warm muffin wrapped in a napkin as she passed by. Every day since she'd returned home, he had coffee and a treat waiting for her as she left for work. What a wonderful way to start the day.

The drive to work gave Juliet a moment to reflect

on the picture in her purse. Was this man her biological father? What did that make Ronald, the only
man she'd ever called "Father"? Should she even
pursue this? Did she really want to know? Yes. She
did. She had to.

She felt a tad guilty for not telling her sisters
about the photo and her suspicions, but she wanted
to have all her facts before she stirred up any more
chaos. At Blanchard Fabrics, she headed to her
office then buzzed Barbara.

"Yes?" Barbara answered the phone.

"Have you heard from my…father? Has he said
when he'll return?"

"No to both questions, Juliet."

"Thanks." She hung up, and then spun her chair
around to look out the small, high window. Gray
clouds skittered across the sky. She was actually
glad that Ronald and Alannah weren't planning on
returning soon. That would give her time to do
some investigating without having to deal with him.
She couldn't guess how he'd react if she came to
him with the news that she wasn't his biological
daughter. Would he be angry? Deny it? Be relieved?

The biggest question was, did he already know?

She pulled the photo from her purse and traced
the images with her finger. First on her agenda was
to visit the college where her mother and the mysterious Arthur had had their picture taken.

Barbara would get suspicious if Juliet just left

without an explanation. Juliet was sure Barbara had orders to keep Ronald posted about how well or not well Juliet was adjusting to her job. Barbara's loyalties were firmly attached to Ronald.

Would Brandon cover for her?

He had no emotional involvement in her family history. And she needed an ally. But was the tentative bond they'd formed enough to tempt him into jeopardizing his own job with Blanchard Fabrics?

Though it wasn't as if she was asking him to do something that would hurt the company. She just needed him to keep her absence quiet while she drove out to the college. Maybe there was an errand that needed to be done for the ad campaign that she could take care of while she was out. Yes. That would be a good cover.

Putting the photo in the pocket of her long, powder-blue duster, she went in search of Brandon. She found him in the conference room. Spreadsheets littered the big, oval table.

"What's up?" she asked as she leaned over his shoulder as he studied the company's financial reports. She picked up the top sheet, noticing that the company was operating in the red. A fissure of alarm tightened her chest. The company could be in trouble and her father was gallivanting around, having a grand time in Europe?

Brandon took the paper from her hands. "Good morning, Juliet. What can I do for you?"

"What do you make of this?" Her voice betrayed her concern.

He returned the sheet to the table. "There have been overexpenditures in some areas that need to be taken care of. We're not utilizing some of our resources as best we could. Nothing to worry about." His gaze lifted and trapped hers. "Thank you for a wonderful evening last night." He abruptly shifted gears. "Your family is very engaging."

The compliment pleased her and smoothed the edges of her worry for the company. "Thank you," she said. "Was everything okay?"

He frowned. "What?"

"The personal business."

"Oh." His smile didn't quite reach his eyes. "Not yet. But it will be."

Biting her lip, her mind fluttered anxiously to the reason she'd sought him out. "Speaking of personal business." Hoping she was doing the right thing by trusting him, she continued, "I have a favor to ask of you."

His mouth quirked in a half grin. "A favor. That sounds interesting."

"I have to leave for a bit. I just want to make sure that if Barbara asks about me, you tell her you sent me on an errand or something."

He eyebrows rose. "You want me to lie to her?"

Ouch! "No. I take that back. Just tell her…I don't know…that I'm out on company business."

"And would you be on company business?"

Her shoulders drooped. "No." What could he say that wouldn't be a lie but would keep Barbara from wanting to know what Juliet was up to?

"What's so important you need to skip out on work to do?"

Brandon's softly asked question brought Juliet's gaze to him. She was bursting with the need to tell someone what she'd discovered. They were friends and she trusted him more than most anyone else who wasn't family.

And if he knew, he would probably be more likely to help her. Taking the picture from her pocket, she held it out for him to see. "I need to find this man."

She watched him examine the picture, look at her and then back at the images on the photo. "Is this your mother?"

"Yes. That was taken before I was born."

"Wow, you *do* look a lot like her."

"What?" His tone suggested he'd had his doubts that she resembled her mother. Why?

He tapped the photo with his finger. "And the man is…"

Refocusing her attention on the picture, she said, "That's what I need to find out."

His gaze searched her face. "Why?"

She tugged at her bottom lip with her teeth as she debated telling him the whole, sordid truth. Having a friend to confide in and help her process what she knew sounded wonderful.

But was Brandon that person? Could she trust him completely?

# SIX

Juliet admitted to herself that ever since she'd met Brandon she'd felt drawn to him.

Even being angry that he'd shown up at the factory as her boss hadn't lessened the compelling pull he had on her. If anything, working with him over the last few weeks had strengthened a connection between them.

She'd already placed her trust in him by asking for his help; might as well jump in with both feet.

Taking a deep breath and praying her trust wasn't misplaced, she told him about the evidence that Bianca and Portia had discovered that revealed there was a chance that Trudy Blanchard hadn't died as everyone believed, but had been living in a mental institution.

A muscle jumped in his jaw.

"I want to find this man to see if he knows anything about her disappearance and—" her voice caught "—and what exactly his relationship was to my married mother."

At his continued silence, she added, "My birthday is exactly ten months after this photo was taken."

She flipped the picture over so Brandon could see the date written on the back.

His eyes widened.

She could see he'd made the same connection she had and she felt slightly better knowing that she wasn't the only one to jump to a conclusion that rocked her world.

He whistled low through his teeth. "Have you asked anyone at the college if they know him?"

She shook her head.

"Though the chances of someone remembering him after twenty-plus years are pretty slim."

"I realize that, but I have to try. Only, if Barbara finds out and tells my father I skipped out on work, he'll be furious."

Brandon's eyes took on a gleam. "She can't ask me a question if I'm not here. And if you're with your boss, how could she say you weren't working?"

She hadn't expected that and wasn't sure how she felt about his offer. Did she want him tagging along? "You'd be willing to come with me? I don't think you have to do that. I mean, what about the ad campaign? Just covering for me would be helpful."

"No. I'll come with you. And I finished up the campaign this morning when I came in. It's ready for Monday."

He'd come in early and worked without her? Had last night made him not want to work so closely? But if that were the case then… She narrowed her eyes. "Why do you want to come?"

He took her hand, sending ribbons of awareness up her arms. "Because it's obvious you're upset by this photo. And I don't think it's wise for you to go searching for answers from the past on your own."

"You sound like my sisters," she huffed, but she couldn't deny that having him along would be a comfort for her sisters when they found out what she'd been doing. Since her sisters didn't think her capable, they'd be glad to know Brandon was tagging along. She agreed for her sisters' sake and she'd refuse to think about the comfort his presence would bring to her. Nothing but trouble in that direction.

"Your sisters love you," he stated with a look in his brown eyes that clearly said she shouldn't be questioning their motives.

"I know, I know. And I'll get less flak if you come with me. Thank you."

"How about we head over to the college for lunch? I hear the café on campus makes a very good Reuben."

She grinned. "That's a wonderful idea."

At noon they drove to the college in Brandon's

SUV. The road leading to the school meandered through wooded land on one side and the Atlantic on the other. The campus was relatively small, though the school had a good academic reputation. The four buildings spaced apart and bordered by lush lawns had old-world charm with redbrick exteriors and white pillars.

In the administration office, modernization could be seen in the gleaming tiled floors and modern built-in counters. Juliet and Brandon approached the young woman manning the desk.

"Hello. We're hoping you could help us," Brandon said in a charming voice that had Juliet doing a double take.

"I'll do what I can." The woman, a brunette in her late twenties, didn't even glance at Juliet but fixed Brandon with a look of invitation that, surprisingly, set Juliet's teeth on edge.

Brandon took the picture from Juliet's hand and held it up. "We're looking for the man in this photo."

The woman glanced at the photo and then back at Brandon. "He doesn't look familiar. Is he a student or a teacher?"

Brandon leaned on the counter. "We're not sure. Any way to find out?"

She peered at the picture. "You know, that's a faculty badge sticking out of his pocket." She handed the photo back. Juliet snatched it from

Brandon's hand and studied Arthur again. Sure enough, there was something sticking out of his front pocket. Why hadn't she noticed it before? Not that she'd have known it was a faculty badge.

The brunette leaned on the counter. "You could try Priscilla Ryder, the dean's secretary. She's been here forever."

"Where do we find her?" Juliet asked.

The woman barely slanted her a glance. "Priscilla is on the fourth floor of this building."

"Great," Brandon said while slipping his arm around Juliet and propelling her toward the elevator.

"Anytime," the woman called after them.

Trying to repress the possessiveness clawing at her but doing a poor job of it, Juliet mimicked, "Anytime." She rolled her eyes. "Ha! She is a fawning, dizzy-eyed, flap-dragon."

Brandon laughed. "What was that? Dizzy-eyed? Flap-dragon?"

Regaining control of her senses, Juliet grinned. "I thought you knew Shakespeare?"

"What play was that from?"

"Don't know. Delia once made a list of all the ways Shakespeare insulted people. We had great fun as kids spouting off insults and no one even realized they were being insulted."

"Clever," Brandon said with appreciation lacing his words.

They stepped out of the elevator on the fourth floor. The dean's offices were at the far end. A seventyish, trim and prim gray-haired woman sat at an L-shaped desk. A brass nameplate with the words *Ms. Ryder* sat facing outward. Behind her were rows of filing cabinets, several thriving potted plants and a row of elegantly framed photos of past deans. Ms. Ryder looked up as they approached.

Her gaze flickered over them with cool appraisal. "Good afternoon. How can I help you?"

Brandon gave Juliet a little nudge with the hand he held at the small of her back, indicating she should proceed.

Juliet smiled, took her cue. "I sure hope you can help. I'm looking for the man in this photo."

Ms. Ryder took the picture Juliet offered, studied it, turned it over and then handed the photo back to Juliet. "Why?"

Juliet swallowed to loosen the knot in the back of her throat. "The woman in this picture is my mother. I want to ask this man some questions about her. You see, she died right after I was born."

Ms. Ryder remained silent for a tense moment. The woman's unemotional gaze unnerved Juliet; she fidgeted with her purse. Finally, Ms. Ryder stood and moved to a filing cabinet, opened a bottom drawer and pulled out a file. Not moving back to the desk, she thumbed through the folder, paused to read something, closed the file and replaced it back in the cabinet. She sat back in her chair, folded her hands on the desktop and stared at Juliet in serene calmness.

Juliet's impatience mounted.

Ms. Ryder nodded her coiffed head toward the photo still in Juliet's hand. "I remember your mother. Trudy Blanchard, correct?"

Juliet nodded. Of course the wife of the Blanchard heir attending school would be noteworthy.

Ms. Ryder's expression softened a fraction. "You have her eyes. The man in the photo with her was a guest instructor that year. His name is Arthur Sinclair."

Sinclair. The name had a romantic flair. Trying to keep her anxious bubbles from spilling all over the place, Juliet asked, "Do you know where he is now?"

Ms. Ryder shook her head. "Mr. Sinclair left after the term and I have not heard of him since. I'm sorry I couldn't be more help."

Juliet's shoulders drooped. Another dead end.

"You've given us a name to work with," Brandon stated.

"Yes, you have," Juliet agreed. "Thank you."

Outside of the administration building, Brandon asked, "Do you want to head to the café?"

Food was the last thing she wanted. "Do you mind if we skip it?"

"Not at all. We'll swing through the drive-through on the way back."

True to his word, Brandon drove through the first fast-food place they came to. Juliet had no appetite. Brandon, however, had no problem eating a hamburger and driving. As they headed toward Blanchard Fabrics, Juliet stared at the photo. "A guest lecturer. Well, now I know why his picture wasn't with the rest of the faculty in Mother's yearbook. Do you think he's still teaching?"

"With any luck," Brandon responded.

"You can't rely on luck in life. God is in control and I'm praying He'll lead us to m—" She paused, not daring to say aloud the suspicion that lurked at the back of her mind. "Mr. Sinclair and some answers."

Brandon slanted a sideways glance in her direction. "You can pray, and I'll cross my fingers."

She leaned her elbow on the armrest of the door and shifted to better study him. "What turned you off of God?"

"What makes you think I was ever turned on to Him?"

"Good point. But there was something that night we first met…I received the distinct impression you had faith once." She shrugged. "I guess I was wrong."

Sadness and a bit of disappointment shot through her. His lack of faith was just one more thing in a long list of reasons why she could never have a romantic relationship with him. She really liked him and had come to trust him in a way she hadn't trusted anyone in a long time. But she knew what

God's word said about becoming involved with a nonbeliever. There couldn't be true unity in their relationship if they were approaching life from opposite beliefs.

"Not completely wrong. My dad was a strong believer."

Her spirit perked up. So there was hope that some seeds of faith had been planted in Brandon. But was she the one to water them? Was that even an option?

She mulled that thought over as they arrived back at the factory.

"Let's go to my office and search the Web for Sinclair," Brandon said as he opened the door of the building for her.

"Good idea." They went to his office, which had a nice corner window with a view of the lush woods surrounding the factory. An expansive desk with a nice leather manager's chair and a large bookcase filled with books were so in contrast to the closet-like office she had been given that Juliet sighed, not with envy as much as wistfulness.

Though to be honest with herself, she'd much rather have a room with easels, sewing machines and mannequins draped in rich fabrics than a corner office with a view. That dream would definitely have to wait until her mother's mystery was resolved.

Brandon sat down at his computer and Juliet

hitched a hip on the armrest of the leather chair, bumping against his shoulder. The point of contact sent a shiver up her spine but her focus remained on the big, flat monitor as Brandon deftly found what they were looking for.

Arthur Sinclair's picture appeared on the Web site of UC Berkeley's staff directory. He was now a professor at the prestigious college in California. They weren't able to find any personal information on him, though. His home phone was unlisted.

They called the faculty number on the Web site's directory and got the recording. Juliet hung up without leaving a message. This was too big to do over the phone.

"Looks like I'm headed to the West Coast." Juliet stood, keyed up by the anticipation of finding Mr. Sinclair.

"Not alone." Brandon sat back, the expensive fabric of his suit stretched across his shoulders as he folded his arms over his broad chest.

"Oh, really?" She glared at him and imitated his posture and tapped a foot. Everybody wanted to boss her around. "Who says you have a say in this?"

"You did, the minute you asked me to cover for you." He rose, tall and forbidding. "Look, Juliet. I get that you don't want your father to know what you're doing. I assume that also includes your sisters, right?"

"Right." She wasn't about to say anything until

she had something of worth to say. If this turned out to be nothing, then keeping her activities quiet wouldn't cause her sisters any undue worry. Not to say she couldn't expect a scathing lecture from each and every one once they did find out she'd gone on a wild-goose chase.

But if she *did* discover something…

Her heart hammered against her ribs. If she discovered something embarrassing about her mother, then she could prepare her sisters before telling them.

"So, that leaves me to accompany you," Brandon said, softly drawing her attention.

She stared into his eyes, not sure what she saw there, some confusing mix of concern and determination. She couldn't deny that traveling to the other side of the country to face a man who may or may not be her father was daunting and overwhelming. Having Brandon's steady strength and confidence to lean on wouldn't be a bad thing. And when her sisters learned what she'd been up to, at least she could assure them she'd been responsible enough not to go alone.

But was accepting Brandon's company on this journey the responsible choice? Especially when she was so attracted to him, no matter how much she tried to deny it?

Relying on the friendship and trust they'd built over the last few weeks, she inclined her head.

"That leaves you. How will we explain our absence to Barbara?"

"We'll make it a business trip. There are two companies in the Bay Area that would be beneficial to visit," he said easily.

That sounded reasonable. "Okay. But we can't tell her until after we've left or she'll call the family and then...forget it." She slashed a hand across her neck in a cutting motion, indicating what would metaphorically happen to them if her sisters found out before she left. No way would they approve of her going on this search.

"Agreed." Brandon checked his watch. "I have a meeting with Jefferies in sales in about twenty minutes. Let's wrap up anything that can't wait until Monday. If we take the first flight out in the morning, we should be able to make it to the school by two, three at the latest."

Juliet put her hand on his arm. The muscles beneath her palms were hard and solid. "Thank you."

"My pleasure." He covered her hand with his.

His masculine, blunt fingers with neatly trimmed nails caressed her hand. Warmth flowed up her arm. She should withdraw from the contact, but she couldn't seem to form the command. She wanted to rotate her hand so their palms were touching and she could entwine her fingers around his.

Taking a deep breath, she finally managed to

bring her mind under control and extracted her hand from beneath his. "We should go to the airport from here in the morning."

His gaze sparked with a bit of confusion and something else she couldn't identify as he stepped back. "Good idea. I'll let you know the flight specifics before you leave today."

With a nod, she left his office and hurried to her own. One way or another, this trip west was going to upset the balance of her life. She had a feeling that an unlikely source—Brandon—was going be her anchor in the storm that was brewing.

Brandon cleared his calendar and made the arrangements for their flight to San Francisco. He couldn't deny the surprised pleasure coursing through him that she would turn to him for help. And that she'd told him, a virtual stranger, their family secrets spoke volumes about the trust she placed in him.

An uncomfortable twinge of guilt played at his conscience. He'd come to Blanchard Fabrics intending to take back the company that rightfully belonged to his family. Yet, with each passing day he'd become more attached to Juliet. And after last night, spending time with the Blanchard women, he felt even more conflicted about his purpose.

It didn't help that his uncle had left town again without a word. Brandon wanted to question his uncle more fully about the feud between the two families. Brandon had his own reasons for wanting revenge on the Blanchards, but when it came to Juliet and the other women, he couldn't find within himself the heartless sense of vengeance that he'd clung to over the years.

So for now, he would commit to helping Juliet, stay as emotionally distant as possible and focus on how this current scenario could work to his advantage. Because ultimately, it was Ronald Blanchard, not Juliet, that Brandon wanted to destroy.

He had a feeling that whatever he and Juliet uncovered would be ammunition he could use.

Juliet slipped from her bed at one o'clock in the morning, wrapped herself in a fleece robe and plodded downstairs. The dark gloominess of the house barely registered. Her mind was too chaotic. She hadn't been able to speak to Brandon before coming home from the office earlier. He'd left her a voice mail saying he'd arranged everything and to meet him at the factory at five in the morning tomorrow. Which was today. In four hours.

Making her way by feel to her father's office, she went to the desk, flipped on the small desk lamp and dialed Brandon's home number, which she'd obtained from Leslie in Human Resources before leaving work today.

As the phone rang, she sank into her father's over-stuffed leather executive chair and propped her elbows on the desk. Her long hair, swept back into a braid, slid over her shoulder and pooled on the desk.

"Hello?" Brandon's groggy voice finally came through the line.

"I can't believe you can sleep," she groused. She hadn't realized how much just hearing his voice would calm her and at the same time send anxious butterflies swarming through her. Uh-oh.

"Juliet? It's one in the morning. What are you doing?"

She flipped her braid back and confessed, "I couldn't sleep."

"So you thought you'd wake me up, too?"

She smiled at the amusement in his voice. "Yeah, something like that."

"Our flight leaves at six-fifteen. We'll arrive in San Francisco close to 1:00 p.m. and rent a car."

She liked that he knew what she needed to hear without having to ask. "How long is the drive from the San Francisco Airport to Berkeley?"

"Forty minutes or so, depending on traffic. I left our return flight open, just in case it takes longer at the school than we anticipate."

She leaned back in the chair, her nerves stretching taut at the thought of meeting Arthur Sinclair. "That's probably a good idea. I don't know—" She stopped as a shadow, darker than the gloom of the house, passed by the doorway. The hairs on the back of her neck rose. She shivered. "Just a sec."

She put the receiver down and rushed to the doorway, then reached around the corner and flicked on the hall light. The hall was empty. She listened and heard nothing unusual. No soft whisper of footsteps or creak of the stairs. Nothing. She rubbed at the goose bumps prickling her arms. Leaving the hall light on, she went back to the phone.

"Sorry about that," she said into the receiver.

"What happened? What's wrong?"

His concern touched her. "Nothing. Just my nerves getting to me. I'll let you get back to sleep. See you in the morning."

"Hey, Juliet?"

"Yes?"

"Pack an overnight bag."

"An overnight bag?" Juliet squeaked.

"Just in case it takes longer than we expect. But I promise, separate hotel rooms," he added with a dose of humor lacing his voice.

She swallowed. "Sure. Okay. Good night."

After she hung up, she hurried back to her room and left the dark house behind her. She shouldn't feel so much anticipation about this trip; it was sure to bring some heartache or disappointment, but she couldn't help looking forward to spending the time with Brandon away from the office.

* * *

In the darkened room, the muffled sound of a phone ringing jerked the woman to her feet. She scuttled to the small, square table and grabbed the handset before another muted sound could break the silence.

"Yes," she said in a low, crisp tone.

"She's leaving town." The voice on the other line sounded hushed, as if the person didn't want to be overheard.

"Destination?"

"California."

The woman gritted her teeth. There was only one reason the brat would go there. The same reason she'd gone to the school yesterday.

Stupid girls! Why couldn't they leave well enough alone? First Bianca, then Portia, snooping where they didn't belong. Now this one? Stupid, stupid, stupid.

The woman pushed her blond hair back from her eyes with an impatient swipe. "If you hear anything else, you call me."

"What about my money?"

Greedy pig! "You'll get it. Same as last time."

The woman hung up and paused a moment, letting the darkness settle around her, giving her anger free rein. So many things stood in the way of what she wanted. But slowly and thoroughly she would eliminate all threats. Nothing and no one would keep her from her ultimate prize.

She knew what to do, who to call. She dialed and waited. The line was picked up on the third ring. "Yeah?"

"I have a job for you," the woman said.

"Target?"

"I'll fax you a picture with details. Make it look like an accident. I don't want the brat coming back."

# SEVEN

The cross-country trip to California from Maine proved uneventful. Juliet enjoyed Brandon's company as they worked on a crossword puzzle together, watched a movie and chatted about life. Anything to keep her mind off the impending meeting with a man who might be her biological father… She didn't start feeling nervous until they hit Berkeley. What was she about to discover?

Brandon drove the rental car through the California traffic as if he'd been doing it his whole life. People were sure in a hurry on the West Coast. At least while they were in their cars.

Brandon drove, following the directions the rental agent had given them to UC Berkeley. The campus was lush and tranquil amid an urban setting with neoclassic buildings spread out among the acres of land that comprised the university. The rolling, green hills of Tilden Regional Park provided a border on one side of the campus while the culturally diverse and politically adventurous city of Berkeley was located nearby.

Signs directed them to the main parking lot. As soon as they parked and climbed from the car, Brandon asked a passing student for directions to the lit building. From their research on the Internet, they knew that Arthur Sinclair taught literature.

As they fell into step, Juliet mused, "And who says guys don't ask for directions?"

Brandon flashed her a grin. "I'm all about expediency. No sense in running in circles when a straight line will get you there faster."

They found the building easily and again asked a passing student where they'd find Professor Sinclair's room. When they approached it on the third floor of the impressive building, the room was dark and empty. They found his office closed up, as well.

"Now what?" Juliet moaned as she slumped against the locked door. "We've come all this way and he's not here."

Brandon took her by the arm and led her back toward the stairs. "Don't give up so easily. Maybe he's in a different lecture hall or in the staff lounge."

Thankful for the boost in morale, Juliet quickened her pace. She just wanted to find the professor and get this over with before she had a hole in her aching stomach from all the nervous acid.

The administration office was extremely busy. Several students waited in chairs lining the wall. Juliet and Brandon stood in line behind a tall African-American man. Juliet fidgeted with her bracelets as they waited. Beneath her breath she said a litany of prayers telling God how scared and nervous she was and how she needed His calming peace.

Finally, they approached the desk. A heavyset woman with large brown eyes and long, dark hair smiled at them. "May I help you?"

"Hi." Brandon smiled back at the woman. "We're looking for Professor Sinclair. His room is locked. Could you tell me where on the campus we could find him?"

The woman scrunched up her nose for a moment. "Hmm. I think he takes Fridays off, but let me verify that." She disappeared into an office.

Juliet sagged against the counter. "Great. We should have thought about that before flying out here."

Brandon's mouth curved in a wry slant. "I did as soon as we got off the phone at one this morning. But it was too late by then." He reached out and tucked some stray hair behind her ear, sending a fissure of warmth along her skin. "We're here and we'll accomplish our task."

She wished she could be as certain. She was so grateful for Brandon's steady confidence and assertiveness. His care and concern touched her deeply.

The woman returned and gave them an apologetic smile. "I'm sorry. Professor Sinclair won't be back on campus until Monday."

"Would you be able to give me his home phone number?"

The woman shook her head. "I'm sorry. We don't give out personal information on our staff."

"I understand," Brandon said. "But we've come all the way from Maine to talk with him. Could you make an exception?"

"I'm afraid not," she said.

"Would you be willing to call him yourself and tell him Trudy's daughter needs to speak with him? He'll understand," Brandon coaxed.

Still, the woman refused.

Juliet fought back tears of frustration. What a waste of time. There was no way she could stay in California until Monday. Her sisters would go nuts with worry.

She and Brandon walked in silence from the administration building. Brandon stopped at the pay phone, thumbed through the phone book. Finding nothing there, he called information on his cell phone and confirmed Professor Sinclair was not listed.

"Excuse me." A girl who had been sitting in one of the chairs came hurrying after them. "Professor Sinclair attends Arbor Community Church."

Juliet blinked. "Are you sure?"

The redheaded girl nodded. "My parents and I attend the church, too, and I've seen Professor Sinclair there several times."

Juliet shifted her gaze to Brandon as she digested the girl's words. Arthur Sinclair was a believer. They would be able to see him on Sunday. This meant they'd have to stay *two* nights in California.

Her sisters were going to have a fit.

Brandon thanked the girl and then hustled Juliet back to the rental car. As she slid into the passenger's seat, Brandon once again had his cell out and was calling information for the number to the church. Soon he was talking with someone there who also refused to give out information on a member of their congregation.

Another roadblock. Juliet leaned back against the headrest, debating whether to call home and explain or wait. Of course, she'd have to call home. She dug out her cell phone. No service. "Can I use your phone to call home?"

"Here." He handed it over.

She dialed the phone, sat searching for a network to connect to. "How come you were able to make calls earlier?"

He shrugged. "I guess because I made local calls."

Flipping the phone closed, she set it in the center console and slanted a glance at Brandon.

His strong jaw was clamped tight and his gaze steady on the road.

Her mind jumped to the kiss they'd shared in front of her house. Who would have guessed he'd kiss so sweetly?

A little thrill raced over her limbs. She was going to have to stay the weekend in California with Brandon.

Separate rooms, of course.

She didn't think even that would mollify her sisters.

Boy, was she in trouble.

Since Berkeley was so close to San Francisco, they decided to stay in the city. Brandon figured the more distractions for Juliet, the better, given how anxious she was and would become as they waited for Sunday.

He found a well-known hotel near Pier 39 and secured two rooms across the hall from each other.

At her room, Juliet slid her electronic key through the lock and pushed the door open. She paused before entering. "Thank you, Brandon, for doing all this."

Her big green eyes stared at him so earnestly that a lump formed in his chest. "You're welcome. How about in two hours we find a restaurant?"

She gave him a tired smile. "Perfect."

"Call your family and let them know, okay? They'll worry otherwise."

"All right."

Brandon watched her slip inside her room, her bright colored skirt swishing softly. The door closed silently behind her.

He entered his own room, decorated in standard hotel colors of blue and gold. After he put his overnight bag on the luggage stand, he sat on the bed and ran a hand through his hair. This unexpected twist in their plans set Brandon's nerves on fire. How was he going to keep an emotional distance from Juliet when they would be alone for the weekend in the city by the bay where romance was practically unavoidable?

"Miss Blanchard!" Sonya Garcia, the Blanchard family's longtime housekeeper bustled her heavyset frame into the dining room. Her perpetual scowl was marred by the worry in her dark, probing eyes.

"What's the matter, Sonya?" Winnie asked, setting down her napkin. A sense of foreboding plucked at her nerves. Rarely were Sonya's feathers ruffled, but obviously something had her in a dither.

With a quick glance at Miranda, who sat opposite to Winnie at the table as they waited for breakfast to be served, Sonya lifted her chin and said, "It's Miss Juliet. She is not here."

Foreboding turned to anxiety and concern. When Juliet had called yesterday, she'd said she'd be working late into the night with Brandon and not to worry. Well, it was unseemly for an unmarried woman to stay the night with a man, even if it was for work and in the workplace.

*Please, Lord, don't let it be too late to keep Juliet from doing something she'll regret.* Winnie grimaced. How many times had she talked to the girls about the importance of staying pure until they were married? They knew God wanted life to be that way. And Winnie had tried to make each of her nieces see that chastity before marriage was a safeguard not meant to rob them of pleasure, but to protect them from taking baggage from a past relationship into their marriages. She despaired that she'd failed at that endeavor.

"You don't think anything bad could have happened to her?" Miranda asked, her golden-brown eyes searching Winnie's for reassurance.

Winnie settled her own thoughts and gave Miranda an encouraging smile. "Of course not. Juliet said she'd be working late. She probably fell asleep on the couch in your father's office. I'll call the factory and wake her."

Sonya sniffed with disdain and muttered, "That girl is a wild one."

Winnie patted Sonya's arm as she passed her. "But we love her."

Sonya's nod may have appeared grudging, but Winnie knew the truth. Sonya loved all the Blanchard women and clucked over them like a mother hen. Winnie had suspected that her father, Howard, and Sonya had once had an affair, but the situation had never become public, and Winnie was thankful. It was hard to teach the girls moral standards when the men in the family weren't any type of role model.

In Ronald's office, Winnie dialed first Juliet's cell number and was immediately put through to her voice mail. She left a message for Juliet to call ASAP. Then Winnie dialed Ronald's private office number. The phone rang and rang. Frowning, Winnie then tried Juliet's extension, but to no avail. She tried Brandon's, as well, and was unrewarded. Anxiety built in her chest as she dug out Barbara Sanchez's home number.

"Hello?"

"Barbara, Winnie Blanchard here. I'm trying to track down my niece. She and Brandon were to have worked late last night but no one is picking up the line in the offices. Would you happen to know Brandon's cell number or home number?"

"Oh, my. I don't have it here at home. I could drive over to the office," Barbara offered, concern evident in her tone.

Winnie waved away that idea. "I can do that. I just thought perhaps…well, I'll go do that."

"If it helps, I do know he rented an apartment in the Highland Building."

"Thank you. Don't worry. I'm sure Juliet will turn up. She always does."

Barbara gave a small laugh. "Yes, that one and Delia always have given Ronald a run for his money."

Winnie agreed and then said goodbye.

Miranda came into the hall as Winnie was putting on her coat. Her delicate hands fidgeted with anxiousness. "Is everything okay? Did you locate Juliet?"

"Not yet," Winnie replied, careful to keep her voice even so she wouldn't worry Miranda unnecessarily.

"I can't believe she hasn't called this morning. What could she be thinking?"

Winnie had the same question running through her mind. "I'm going to drive to the factory," Winnie said. "Would you like to come?"

Miranda backed up a step. "No."

Winnie hadn't expected her to agree to accompany her but she always tried, hoping one day Miranda would overcome her agoraphobia. "I'll let you know as soon as I find her."

Miranda nodded and swept back into the dining room. Winnie heard her humming a lullaby that Trudy had sung to the children. Miranda always fell back on that tune when she was stressed or upset. Winnie was going to give Juliet a good talking-to for causing this bit of drama.

Winnie drove her sedan through town as fast as

the law allowed. At the factory, she found the doors to the building locked and the place dark. Juliet's car sat in the parking lot. Where was that girl?

Hoping the suspicion running through her mind was wrong, Winnie drove to the Highland Building. The top two floors of the newly constructed semi-high-rise were made up of apartments. After sweet-talking the doorman, Winnie was directed to Brandon's apartment on the top floor. With a purposeful stride, she exited the elevator and came to a stop in front of Brandon's door. She rapped her knuckles on the wood just below the gold numbers.

The door swung open. A ruggedly handsome man in his midsixties, wearing a stylish polo shirt and chinos, filled the door frame. His gray eyes first regarded Winnie with surprise before turning to icy steel.

Winnie blinked, sure she was hallucinating. But she wasn't. Before her stood the lost love of her life.

Tate Connolly.

Tate stared at the woman who'd been wrenched from his life so many years ago.

Winnie stared back, her eyes still as stunning as they'd been when he'd met her during their boarding school days in Switzerland. In fact, age had taken the once sweet-faced and charming young girl and turned her into a strikingly attractive woman. Her vibrant red hair may have lost some of its glow but his hand itched to loosen the elegant roll at the nape of her slender neck. He liked the classical lines of her stylish pantsuit that hugged her medium-height frame in an appealing way. A dizzying sense of elation warred with the bitter anger he'd nurtured all these years. The anger knocked the elation aside and won out. "What do you want?"

"What…what are you doing here?" she asked, her voice cracking a bit.

Tate leaned against the doorjamb and crossed his arms over his chest, not so much as to be intimidating but to hide the slight paunch in his midsection. Funny how he'd never given the condition of his physique any thought until he'd opened the door to Winnie Blanchard. "I'm visiting my nephew."

The minute the words were out he regretted them as apprehension rippled through him that his and Brandon's plans for revenge may be thwarted.

Her eyes grew wide, emphasizing the kaleidoscope of colors in the hazel orbs. "You're Brandon's uncle?" A thoughtful expression settled on her features. "That makes sense. I thought he seemed familiar. He looks so much like you did at that age."

Tate arched an eyebrow as pleasure washed over him. "You remember what I looked like?"

She blushed becomingly. "Of course. I have many fond memories of that time in my life."

He did, too, right up until Howard and Ronald Blanchard had stepped in and effectively destroyed the budding romance between him and Winnie, and she'd gone along with it. "What do you want with my nephew?"

"Is Brandon here?"

"No."

Concern etched fine lines at the creases of her mouth. "Do you know where he is?"

Tate frowned. "No."

His nephew hadn't been home last night when Tate returned from attending to some business in Chicago. Tate had assumed Brandon had gone away for the weekend for some R & R. But now that Winnie was standing at his door asking for the boy, Tate realized how unlikely it was that his workaholic nephew would take off when they were in the midst of their plans for revenge. "What's going on, Winnie?"

She reached up to twirl a diamond stud earring in her ear, a nervous habit Tate remembered. A diamond his family's company had paid for.

Her forehead furrowed. "My niece and your nephew both seem to be missing."

Tate pushed off of the doorjamb. "Come in and sit down so you can explain this to me."

He led Winnie into the stark, ultramodern apartment. All black, white and chrome. Not especially to Tate's liking. He much preferred rustic charm and antiques. Winnie sat on the black leather sofa. Tate took a seat opposite her in an armless chair. The distance was not enough to mute his awareness of her.

"Juliet and Brandon were supposed to be working late last night—" She stopped herself and gave him a quizzing look. "You did know Brandon was working for Blanchard Fabrics, didn't you?"

Tate nodded. Not only did he know, but he'd helped orchestrate the position by enticing the former marketing director away with a position in another company that Tate had a majority of stock in. He needed to tread carefully with Winnie to keep from ruining his plans. "So my nephew and your niece were working late…"

He knew Brandon and Juliet were spending a great deal of time together. Was this a maneuver on Brandon's part to further their plans? Or was he really interested in the youngest Blanchard? Were they even together?

"Yes. Juliet had left a message saying as much. But she was missing this morning. And I went to the factory today. Her car is there but the place is locked up tight."

She wrung her hands with worry. Obviously, she cared deeply for the girl. Did she consider Ronald's kids the children she'd never had? Sadness for what could have been seeped into Tate's heart. They could have been parents together.

"Juliet's not answering her cell phone. I don't know who else to check with. Maybe she went to see Bianca. Or Rissa. I should have thought of that sooner." She gave a curt nod. "Probably Portia." She stood, agitation evident in every line and angle of her being. "I should call Portia right away."

Tate rose, placing a hand on her slim shoulder. "Calm yourself," he said gently. "I'm sure Juliet is fine. You can call Portia from here."

He pulled out his cell phone, flipped it open and handed it to Winnie.

She immediately dialed a number. After a brief conversation with Portia, she hung up. Tate guessed from the worry in Winnie's expression that Portia didn't know where her sister was, either.

His mind running through scenarios, he asked, "You really think Juliet might be with Brandon?"

Winnie sank back onto the sofa. "I'm not sure what to think or hope for. I mean, if they're together then surely she's safe. He seemed like such a nice young man and the fact that he's your nephew is reassuring. But if they're not…" She shuddered.

An overwhelming sense of protectiveness chased by guilt flushed through Tate and he sat beside Winnie, placing an arm around her shoulders. She felt vulnerable beneath his arm. "We'll find them. Both of them."

For a fraction of a second she leaned into his embrace and it seemed as if the pain of the past disappeared and they were young again. Young and in love.

But then Winnie stiffened and pulled away to stand. Tate chastised himself for his romanticism, a weakness to be sure. The past and their relations would always stand between them. And after he and his nephew destroyed Blanchard Fabrics, there would never be a chance for reconciliation between him and Winnie. Regret for what might have been with the only woman he'd ever loved weaseled its way into his heart. He quickly quashed the sentiment.

Better to discover his nephew's plans and figure out how to use this unexpected visit from Winnie to their advantage. He'd simply have to keep his heart on a short leash.

No way would he fall for Winnie Blanchard again.

# EIGHT

Winnie paced across the large, black-and-cream, square art deco floor rug in Brandon's apartment. Her heart and her mind were jumping with so many feelings and emotions, it was hard to hang on to just one. Concern and worry for her niece tightened her lungs. Pleasure, confusion and wariness of Tate Connolly beat a steady rhythm behind her eyes. She should have guessed Brandon and Tate were related.

Though Tate was older and his honey-blond hair had become a distinguished silver and his sun-weathered face showed lines where once there had been none, he was as handsome now as he had been when she'd first met him at the school welcome rally. They'd both been new to Switzerland and the boarding school. The handful of American students had bonded together, though she and Tate grew very close.

He'd been her anchor in a strange land, away from her family and friends. Until…

She tore her mind away from those awful last days in Switzerland and focused on the here and now. Juliet was missing. This was no time to moon over Tate Connolly.

Winnie lifted her chin. "I should go. Maybe she's returned home by now."

"Why don't you call the manor?" Tate suggested.

She did, but Juliet had not returned. Sonya promised to call Winnie's cell when Juliet showed up. "Now what? Where could your nephew have taken Juliet?"

Tate tucked in his chin. "Why do you assume this is Brandon's fault?"

She held up a hand. "I'm just upset."

His expression softened. "I'll call Brandon." He dialed and listened for a moment, then hung up. "Wherever he is, he's not getting cell service. I'll e-mail his PDA," Tate stated as he moved toward a large black desk with a computer. He sat in the black leather chair.

Winnie hurried to his side. "That would be wonderful. Thank you."

Tate rapidly hit the keys on the keyboard and clicked the send button. "It may take a bit before he responds."

He gazed up at her. She was so close she could see the bristles of his beard and smell the faint scent of his aftershave. A spicy, invigorating scent that reminded her of the Alps and young love. She stepped back because the past couldn't be recaptured as easily as a scent.

He rose and strode toward the kitchen. "Coffee?"

"No. I couldn't eat or drink anything right now."

He nodded and poured himself a cup.

An awkward silence seeped between them, filling the air with a tension that was oppressive. Winnie moved to stand by the window. Up high like this, she was able to see for miles. The view of Stoneley, a remarkably beautiful small town with picturesque harbors, rugged peninsulas and majestic lighthouses dotting the landscape should have eased her tension. She loved her hometown, so steeped in history, and the people of Maine, friendly and unassuming.

But Tate's presence, only a few feet behind her, kept her from finding any solace in the view.

A ripple of awareness shot up her spine as Tate joined her at the window.

"Why didn't you ever get married?"

She sucked in a sharp breath at his soft question. "How did you know I never married?"

"Brandon."

How did she tell Tate no man ever measured up to the memories she had of her first love—him? She shrugged, settling for a partial truth. "It never seemed to be right."

In her peripheral vision she saw him nod. Was his acknowledgment understanding or agreement? "What about you? Did you ever get married?"

"No. I didn't." He moved away, effectively cutting off the conversation.

She turned to watch him as he returned to the desk and hit a key on the computer keyboard. He moved with fluid grace that came with confidence and maturity.

He watched the computer screen for a moment, then said, "Here we go."

Winnie hurried over. She read the words on the screen.

Uncle. Everything is under control. Juliet and I are enjoying a bit of a vacation, mixed with some work. We'll talk further when I return. Brandon.

"Work? Vacation?" Winnie shook her head. "Why doesn't Barbara know this? Why didn't Juliet tell her family she was leaving? Something's not right here." Winnie pointed at the screen. "Write him back and tell him to have Juliet call home immediately."

Tate eyed her. "Don't you think that's a bit autocratic?"

Winnie straightened to her full height. "Not in the least. Especially when it concerns one of my girls."

Tate snorted. "*Your* girls? I wonder what good old Ronnie would have to say about that?"

Winnie didn't like the bitter tone in Tate's voice,

but she couldn't think about the significance of that right now. "Please, Tate. I just need to hear Juliet's voice."

His expression softened. "Of course, Win." He typed a response.

This time they didn't have to wait. Words appeared on the screen within moments of Tate's pushing Send.

I'll tell Juliet.

Winnie blinked back tears of frustration.

"Hey, now. Brandon wouldn't do anything to hurt Juliet," Tate said as he rose and put a comforting arm around Winnie's shoulders.

For the second time, Winnie allowed herself to melt into his embrace. It had been so long since she'd been held by anyone other than the children. And to have Tate's strong arm encircling her brought a peace she'd been without for a long time.

A peace that had been shattered.

A peace she longed to reclaim.

But how could she? So much lay between them. So many years of heartache.

Gathering her courage and her self-control, she eased away from him. "I'd better get home for when she calls."

The flash of hurt and sadness in his eyes twisted around Winnie's heart. He walked her to the door.

"You'll call me if you hear from Brandon?"

"Yes. And let me know what Juliet has to say."

With a nod and a wave, she walked away. And prayed that, unlike so long ago, she would see Tate again soon.

Brandon stared at his BlackBerry as another message came across the screen from his uncle. This one more pointed and easily conveying his uncle's agitation.

Brandon was surprised to read that Winnie Blanchard had shown up at his condo looking for Juliet. He could only assume that Juliet's family was sick with worry. Yet Brandon understood Juliet's need to do this on her own, without her family's interference.

He would protect her and her privacy. He had no idea why, when it went against everything he'd been planning.

He knew she'd left a message yesterday from the airport that they'd be late, but that was before they'd learned that their trip had to be extended if they were to see Arthur Sinclair. He hadn't thought to ask if she'd called last night when they went to dinner. He'd assumed she had.

Brandon set aside his PDA and finished getting himself ready. Because he'd been able to visit a factory that made dye and a silk import business yesterday while Juliet had rested, today he was determined to show Juliet a good time in the city.

And maybe he could pretend they were just two ordinary people with no family history.

Outside his hotel window, the mild California weather was a welcome change from the wintry March winds in Maine.

He left his room and knocked on Juliet's door. After a moment the door opened and she stepped into the hall wearing jeans tucked into tall, brown leather boots. Over her bright-pink cable-knit turtleneck she had on a cream-colored shearling vest. A matching hat sat perched on her head and a long, blond braid hung over one shoulder. He approved of her look and her wide grin.

"Slept well, did you?" he asked.

She shook her head. "Not a wink. But I'm starved."

He laughed. "Eating's on the agenda, but first, did you call home last night?"

She wrinkled up her nose. "I forgot."

"Convenient," he said drolly.

"They're going to ask questions."

He shrugged. "You gotta do what you gotta do." He held out his handheld.

With a resigned sigh, she dialed. With a triumphant gleam, she announced, "No service."

Slipping the device back into the pocket of his sport coat, he took her by the elbow and led her to his room, then pointed her to the phone on the nightstand.

Making a face, she made the call. "Miranda? Yes, I'm fine."

She closed her eyes as she listened. "I didn't mean to worry anyone. This was sort of last-minute." She sent Brandon a panicked stare. "Where am I?" She winced. "Of course I heard you. She did?" She made another face at Brandon. "Tell Auntie I'm fine and will call again soon."

She listened for a moment more, then said into the phone, "Miranda, I have to go now. Honey, I have to go. Yes. Yes. Okay. I will. I promise." She hung up and quickly dropped the receiver as if it were a snake. "Ugh!"

"That bad, huh?" He followed her back out into the hall.

"Miranda's the oldest and sometimes can be bossy and mothering." Juliet grimaced. "Aunt Winnie went to your place looking for me. I hate to think she believed that you and I…I mean, that we…" She blushed.

Heat crept up his neck because he didn't have a hard time imagining them together. As a couple. Okay, the reality of spending time with Juliet without letting romance interfere was going to be harder than he thought. He started them walking to the elevator. "I'm not sure if I should be insulted or not," he quipped, hoping to keep a light attitude between them.

She slanted him a glance. "*Not*. It's just that Auntie and my father are big on propriety."

"Hmm. You're going to be in big trouble when we get back, aren't you?"

She rolled her eyes. "You have *no* idea."

He was sure he did. Juliet was the baby chick of the flock, and from what he could tell of the other sisters and Winnie, they liked to coddle Juliet even though she didn't want them to. He admired that she didn't succumb to the role of helpless, needy female. She was a capable, smart and passionate woman with a heart of gold. But with a steely determination that would provide the strength to do what she felt was right.

He couldn't ignore the sharp jab of guilt stabbing at his gut. Today he wouldn't think about vendettas or corporate raids or betrayals. Today he was going to enjoy Juliet's company as a friend. He wouldn't allow more, because disaster would only result from such folly.

After a hearty breakfast in the hotel's restaurant, they set out on foot to explore Pier 39. The happy colors of the festival marketplace teeming with crowds of tourists was just the thing to distract Juliet. She beamed as they watched the street performers entertain the crowds. They rode the Venetian Carousel and admired the painted scenes depicting life in Venice.

The best part was watching the sea lions piled like stacks of logs on top of each other, each squirming a bit to gain a better sunning position at the far end of the pier.

They lunched in a popular restaurant on

Fisherman's Wharf overlooking the ocean, where they watched the boats coming and going to Alcatraz. From there they walked to Ghirardelli Square. The brick-terraced courtyards of the once-renowned chocolate factory provided a breathtaking view of the bay.

The *ding, ding* of the cable car grabbed Brandon's attention. He hurried Juliet over to the cable car's turntable, paid the fare and then stepped to the end of the line behind a family with three rambunctious children.

Juliet clapped her hands. "This is great."

Brandon thought *she* was great. Her enthusiasm tickled him. Watching her eyes light up and her beaming smile brought him a deep sense of satisfaction.

"I've always wanted to ride one of these," she said as the line moved forward. "I came to San Francisco once right after high school. Delia met me here. But we didn't take the time to ride the cable car."

"I've ridden it a few times when I've come to the Bay Area on business," Brandon commented. "Here we go."

He offered his hand to her as she stepped up on to the side platform of the car. Since they were near the last to board, Brandon and Juliet stayed standing. The cable car moved forward with slightly jerking motions and a hiss of electrical current ran from the track to the center cable that gripped a long, continuous cable overhead.

"Hang on tight," Brandon cautioned as the car picked up some speed and ambled through the streets of San Francisco. The red car stopped periodically to let passengers off and on.

A seat opened up. Brandon motioned for Juliet to take it, but she shook her head. He didn't blame her wanting to remain standing. The view was much better that way. The architecture of the old Victorian-style buildings was breathtaking, as were the many tall glass buildings rising up from the downtown district.

The car descended one of the many hilly streets as they traveled away from the city's core and another trolley car climbing the hill in the opposite direction approached them. Juliet held on to the overhead bar with one hand and waved as the cars passed each other.

Brandon's gaze followed the car behind them and then snagged on the view of the Pacific Ocean, with its frothy waves on blue-green water. An ocean filled with sharks and sea lions. One couldn't tell what threats lay beneath the surface. Juliet had no idea what threat stood beside her. He was a shark, a corporate raider seeking revenge for something that Juliet had not been involved with.

A sickening repulsion for who he'd become churned in his gut.

Beside him, Juliet bumped against him as the cable car followed a curve in the tracks. He began to turn toward her just as she gasped, then let out a scream.

She was falling.

Brandon reacted instinctively. His arm shot out to grab the back of her vest as she was flung forward, one foot slipping off the step. Brandon pulled her back against his chest, snaking his arm around her middle to steady her while his other hand held tightly to the overhead bar. His heart beat out a frantic rhythm.

"Next stop," he yelled to the gripman, who rode at the very front of the car, to indicate they wanted off.

Juliet trembled as Brandon helped her disembark the car after it came to a stop.

Grabbing her shoulders, he stared into her face. "Are you okay? What happened?"

Her gaze followed the trolley as it continued on its way. "I don't know. I was waving and then someone jostled me. I lost my balance." She turned her wide eyes to him. "Thank you for saving me."

Terror twisted in his gut. "Someone pushed you?"

A crease formed between her eyebrows. "I couldn't tell. It happened so fast. I'm sure it was an accident."

The uncertainty in her eyes conveyed her doubts about the truth of her words.

Breathing deeply to ease his panic and bring his thoughts into some logical order, he refrained from voicing the suggestion that the incident was no accident. The thought of something bad happening to her made everything inside him squeeze tight with icy fear.

He tried to recall who had been close enough to Juliet to have pushed her. He vaguely remembered a couple, young and uninterested in the sights, standing close to her. An older man had sat off to Juliet's left. A book-reading woman had sat directly behind Juliet.

Any one of them had been within striking distance of Juliet. But why would someone want to hurt her?

Protectiveness and anger raged even as the deep caring he felt for Juliet knotted his chest. Though it was crazy and contradicted his own plans for ruining Blanchard Fabrics, he'd do whatever was necessary to keep her safe. Though he doubted his heart would ever be safe from Juliet.

Late that night as Juliet lay in her hotel room and tried to find sleep, she had to admit she was still shaken up by her near fall. If Brandon hadn't grabbed her, she'd have been roadkill for sure.

"Thank You, Lord, for Brandon's quick reflexes," she said aloud, her voice breaking the silence of the darkness.

She'd told Brandon she couldn't tell if she'd been deliberately pushed because she didn't want to believe that someone would be so cruel, but the feel of a hand on her back still burned.

There was no way to find answers to the randomness of what had happened. Better to focus on the good parts of the day.

She'd enjoyed wandering through the many shops of Pier 39 and Ghirardelli Square. Brandon had been a wonderful companion, sweet, fun and kooky. She'd seen a side of him that sent her heart to fluttering.

And tonight as they'd dined in a fancy restaurant in Union Square, he'd had the live band play her favorite jazz song. When he'd walked her to her door, he'd kissed her hand. A sweet gesture of affection.

If every day could be like this one she'd be a happy woman. Assuming no one else tried to shove her from a cable car. She shuddered.

But tomorrow couldn't be put off. She had to find the answers that had propelled her across the country. And then she would think about the future.

A future she hoped could include Brandon. But was affection all that he felt for her?

# NINE

Brandon wove through the early-morning Sunday traffic on the freeway that would take him and Juliet back to Berkeley. He'd found the address of the Arbor Community Church in the phone book. The first service began at ten. He hoped they wouldn't have to sit through two services to find Arthur Sinclair. Brandon hadn't stepped foot in a church since his parents' funeral.

He wasn't looking forward to it now. God had betrayed his father's trust. Now, Brandon didn't trust God.

Beside him, Juliet stared silently out the window. Her mood this morning had been somber and clearly nervous. It didn't help that a light drizzle had begun as they'd left the city, making the day gloomy.

Last night at dinner he'd tried vainly to keep his head and heart from becoming more attached to her.

But he'd failed miserably. When he was with her, she was all he could think about. All he could focus on.

Not smart.

He'd do better today now that the romance of the city would be behind them and they would both be focused on finding her answers.

He'd start by focusing on his driving.

Brandon signaled to change lanes. A black sedan with tinted windows coming up on his right stayed even with the bumper of the rental car. Brandon accelerated, needing to get over to take the next exit, but the other car matched his speed.

Gritting his teeth, Brandon punched the gas pedal and shot forward, cutting in front of the other car to barely make their exit. The sedan kissed the rental car's bumper as it followed them down the off-ramp.

Juliet's gasp echoed the one inside Brandon's head.

He braked as they neared the upcoming intersection and hoped the traffic light remained green because his speed was too fast to stop without skidding or being rear-ended.

They sailed through the intersection just as the light changed to yellow.

Aware of Juliet's anxious stare, he slowed the car to a more reasonable pace. He checked the rearview mirror. The sedan stayed on his tail.

"What's with this guy?" Brandon groused. The

sedan's front windshield was tinted, so Brandon wasn't sure if the driver was male, but the level of aggression made it a good guess.

Juliet turned to look over her shoulder. "I've heard about crazy California drivers, but this is ridiculous."

The street they were traveling climbed a small rise and then evened out as it became an overpass to another busy highway. Behind them, the sedan pulled out into the oncoming lane and sped up. More than willing to let the other car pass, Brandon took his foot off the gas. The sedan pulled alongside them.

"Pass already," Brandon said and applied pressure to the brake. The sedan slowed, too.

They cleared the overpass. A small grouping of trees cropped up along the side of the road. The sedan suddenly swerved toward them as a car approached from the opposite direction.

"Hold on!" Brandon cranked violently on the wheel. The tires squealed on the slick, wet pavement. The sound struck terror in Brandon's soul.

Their car skidded off the road, sending them careening into the trees. He slammed hard on the brakes. The car slid to a stop, barely managing to avoid a head-on with a tree trunk.

Brandon stared straight ahead but the images in his mind were of another time when the car he'd been in hadn't missed the oncoming tree.

Breathing hard, Brandon leaned his head against the headrest and closed his eyes to wipe away the image in his mind. He became aware of Juliet's shallow breaths. Grateful the air bags hadn't deployed, he asked, "You okay?"

She pushed herself back from the dashboard. Her normally rosy complexion had gone pasty white, marred only by a red mark on her forehead. "Other than needing to hurl? I'm okay."

The relief that she hadn't been hurt was intense and so at odds with what he should feel for a member of the Blanchard family.

She opened the door and stumbled out of the car into the muddy terrain. Brandon opened his door and stood, his legs shaking as he scanned the area. They were alone. The sedan was long gone. Had the sedan's intent been to cause their accident or had it been a random bad driver?

He came around the car to find Juliet bent over, her head down, her elbows propped on her knees. Her loose, long hair cascaded toward the ground. Afraid she was about to be sick and dirty her hair, Brandon gathered the silky strands and held them away from her face. He rubbed her back with his free hand.

Slowly, she straightened. He released her hair and steadied her with a hand to her arm. She gripped him tightly.

"Whew. Talk about motion sickness. That was worse than a roller-coaster ride," she said.

"I'm sorry."

"Not your fault some idiot never learned to drive properly. We should call the police or something and get that numskull off the road."

"I didn't catch the license plate, did you?" he asked.

"No, I was too busy praying," she replied.

"I don't think calling the police will do any good." Brandon's gut clenched. On the surface, their near miss with the tree seemed like an accident caused by a lousy driver. But after the scare yesterday on the cable car, Brandon wasn't so sure. He wished he'd had the presence of mind to memorize the license plate.

Someone didn't want Juliet to meet Arthur Sinclair. Why? What answers would she find that would warrant such violence? And would those answers help destroy the Blanchards?

The burning need to avenge his parents' death warred with the love growing in his heart for Juliet.

He groaned. Great. He had fallen for his enemy.

"Hey, you're bleeding!" Juliet exclaimed, pointing to his mouth and chin.

Brandon reached up to find the lower half of his face wet with blood. He pinched the end of his nostrils and tilted his head back. "Nosebleed."

Juliet opened the back door and guided him into the seat. She gave him a tissue and hovered over him. "Did you smack the steering wheel?"

He shook his head.

"Do you get them often?"

"Occasionally. Mainly when stressed."

"This would qualify as stressful. What can I do to help?" She took his hand in hers, the pressure comforting and warm.

"Nothing. It should stop in a few minutes."

"You're shaking." She touched his cheek. "Are you okay?"

Brandon closed his eyes. "This brought back some bad memories."

"The car accident that took your parents' lives?"

Wariness slammed into his gut. He opened his eyes. "How did you know about that?"

"You told me that first night we met."

"Oh. I guess I forgot."

"What happened?"

He took a deep breath and slowly exhaled. "It was raining. Mom was driving. She and Dad were arguing over…some things. She took the turn too fast and overcompensated. The car hit a tree." He didn't mention that they'd been arguing about Blanchard Fabrics after hearing a jingle on the radio.

Juliet's heart contracted in her chest as she involuntarily glanced at the tree just yards away. "You were in the car?"

He nodded.

"Oh, Brandon. I'm so sorry." She laid her head on his chest, wanting to ease the ache she sensed in his soul. Her own soul ached for the little boy who witnessed such tragedy. "That must have been awful. I praise the Lord you were spared."

He shifted. "Praise Him?" He sneered. "He allowed my parents to die."

She raised her head and met his gaze, noting that the bleeding had stopped. "You can't think that way, Brandon. God protected you. As He did just now."

"Why me and not them?"

A deep pain squeezed her heart at the guilt she heard in his tone. "I don't have an answer to that. He has plans for you, Brandon. I do know your parents wouldn't want you to feel guilt for something that was an accident."

"Guilt?" He stared at her as if she'd grown a third eyeball.

"I've read that survivor's guilt is a way of coping, of trying to deal with a sense of helplessness in controlling traumatic events. Did you ever talk to a professional after the accident?"

"No."

"How about your father's pastor?"

"After their funeral, I couldn't…I never went back to church."

A deep sadness welled up, making her heart ache. "At times faith in God is the only thing that has kept my sisters and me sane. In church, I always find His peace."

He scooted away from her and opened the door

on the opposite side and slid out. She followed, hurting even more that he'd shut her out and avoided dealing with his parents deaths.

He moved to the driver's side and slid into the seat. "We'd better go or we'll miss the opportunity to find Arthur Sinclair."

She hated the harsh bitterness etching lines around his mouth. She hated even more that he blamed God for his parents' deaths and felt guilty for surviving. She wasn't sure how to reach him and help him to understand that God loved him then and still did.

The drive to Arthur Sinclair's church was rife with tension. Tension at what was to come, but also tension for what Brandon had revealed. The tension increased as they parked and entered the austere church building. Juliet and Brandon slid into a back pew.

From the outside the church hadn't held much appeal but the inside was rustic and quaint with soothing sage-colored carpet, a wooden altar and a music system that really accentuated the acoustics of the worship music.

Juliet allowed God's presence to fill her. And she prayed that she'd be able to help Brandon find his way to God and help him to come to terms with the trauma of his parents' deaths.

Brandon resisted the peace that tried to rob him of the anger in his soul. But slowly, as the hymns and the word of God washed over him, he began to relax and a calmness he'd never experienced before seeped into him, filling all the dark places.

*God protected you.*

Brandon couldn't understand why God would have protected him and not his parents. Especially his father, a man who tried to follow the teachings of Jesus. What made Brandon more valuable than his parents?

Like a wrecking ball let loose, guilt and frustration and anger shattered the momentary calmness into a million jagged pieces. His chest heaved from the stabbing pain.

He slanted a glance at Juliet. The expression of peace on her pretty face tugged at him. How could she be so faithful and steadfast knowing that soon her life could take an unexpected turn?

Where did that kind of peace come from?

Brandon didn't know. But for the first time in his adult life, he wanted to find out.

Winnie stood on the sidewalk outside of the Beaumont Beanery. On a late Sunday afternoon, the small Maine town had a steady beat of life in the downtown area. A line formed outside the old-fashioned movie house to see the newest comedy offered by Hollywood. Cars lined the street, a telltale sign that the many charming shops were busy with customers. Winnie took a deep breath before entering the coffee shop where she'd agreed to meet Tate.

Did he have news of Juliet? Or was this meeting more personal? Her heart did a little jittery jig, which she tried to ignore as she stepped inside.

Dark timber beams spanned the ceiling and square wooden tables dotted the oak floor. The only colors beyond browns came from gilt-framed pictures, the people and the roaring fire. The aromas of strong coffee and pastries dazzled her senses. She spotted Tate sitting on a plush, caramel-colored chair in the far corner near the stone fireplace. He looked sporty and half his age in his striped polo-style shirt and chinos. She patted the chignon at the nape of her neck then twisted her earring.

She wound her way through the crowded coffee-house and took the seat opposite Tate. His eyes lit up with pleasure. A mug of steaming, rich coffee waited for her, prepared just the way she liked it. He was still as thoughtful now as he had been so many years ago.

He smiled at her, his eyes reflecting the glow of the fire's flames. "You are stunning."

The heat in Winnie's cheeks had nothing to do with the blazing fireplace. Pleasure from his compliment—from his mere presence—sent her heart fluttering. She really had to get control of her emotions and concentrate on why she was here—to find out if he'd heard from his nephew and her niece. "I'm glad you called."

"How was church?"

Setting her handbag aside, she answered, "Very nice. I wish you had joined me."

He gave her a half smile. "Maybe someday."

Winnie took that as a good sign. At least he wasn't totally closed to God. "Have you heard from Brandon and Juliet?"

"No. You?"

"She called and talked with Miranda. And of course, didn't tell Miranda a thing," Winnie huffed.

"I did discover they are in San Francisco. They're booked on a flight home this evening."

A flood of relief at the news relaxed some of the tension in Winnie's shoulders. "Good. The girls are all worried. Bianca and Rissa came home last night. I'm sure they'll stay until Juliet returns safely." She shook her head. "I don't know what Juliet and Brandon were thinking."

She'd hoped Juliet was past the flighty days of her youth, but this little episode clearly showed otherwise. But Brandon had seemed so rock solid.

Tate's eyes took on a speculative gleam. "Maybe they're in love."

Waving away that notion, she said, "No. That couldn't be."

Tate frowned. "And why not?"

She stared, wondering how he could be so obtuse. "He's her boss. Besides, they hardly know each other."

"They probably know each other a lot better after this weekend," Tate commented.

Winnie's insides knotted with anxiety. "I hope you're wrong about that. Juliet may be flighty at times, but she wouldn't do something stupid. And Ronald would be livid."

Folding his arms over his chest, Tate's voice took on a cold edge. "So my nephew's not good enough for your niece? Because he's a Connolly?"

"That has nothing to do with it," she argued.

"Really? It had everything to do with why your family broke us apart."

Old hurt welled up, making Winnie's chest burn. "My father may not have approved of our relationship, but it was you who chose not to fight for us."

"*Excuse me?* I don't think so. You were engaged to another man within weeks after leaving school. Your brother showed me the newspaper clipping of you smiling for the camera on someone else's arm."

Anger sparked white-hot behind her eyes. "The engagement wasn't my idea. And I didn't marry him."

The derisive expression in his eyes mocked her anger. "What happened? Daddy decided *he* wasn't good enough, either?"

Winnie clenched her fist. "I refused to go through with it. Which is more than you can say."

He scoffed. "What's that supposed to mean?"

Ancient pain that was still so fresh sliced across

her heart. "I was all set to defy my father and return to Europe, to you, when my brother showed me the cashed check bearing your signature on it. Our relationship was worth two hundred thousand to you. Appalling. Utterly appalling."

Tate's gaze turned troubled. "I didn't keep that money. I gave it to a homeless shelter. And I wrote to you for a year. You didn't write back."

Winnie stilled. "You wrote to me? Ha! *I* wrote to *you*. But I certainly never heard from you."

Tate's mouth twisted, his bitterness clear. "Your father and brother must have intercepted the letters."

Betrayal sat heavy on her shoulders. "I can't believe they would do such a thing. They both knew how much I loved you. Daddy didn't want to accept it, but I was determined to be with you. Why would he not want me to be happy?"

Tate reached across the table and took her clenched hand. He slowly stroked her skin until she relaxed her fist. "I was a fool not to follow you home."

The hurt and anger she'd harbored in her heart toward him melted. She entwined her fingers around his. Age had cast lines and darkened some areas of their hands but that couldn't lessen the welcome contact. "We were both manipulated."

That was so like her father. He'd spent his whole life trying to control everything and everyone.

Ronald, unfortunately, was following closely in their father's footsteps. It wasn't fair that she and Tate had lost so many years. "Where do we go from here?"

Tate slipped his hand away. "Your father and brother have to pay for what they've done to my family. To us."

Her heart shriveled just a bit. "Revenge is no answer."

"It's all I have left." The granite-hard set to his jaw spoke of his anger and his determination.

Her breath caught, constricting her throat. The fun-loving, carefree young man she'd fallen in love with all those years ago had changed. She swallowed. "But what of love?"

"I…don't know."

A deep, searing pain knifed through her. Was a second chance at love too much to hope for?

# TEN

The service at Arbor Community Church ended. Juliet and Brandon hurried out the door first and stood in a spot where they had a clear view of people streaming out the double doors.

Juliet's breath hitched as a familiar-looking tall, lanky man with graying, wavy black hair stepped through the doors. He paused to adjust his wire-rimmed glasses, his blue eyes visible behind the lenses.

"There he is," Juliet whispered and clutched at Brandon's sleeve.

He nodded and propelled her forward. She suddenly felt a bit shy about approaching this man. He could be her father. What if he didn't have any answers to the questions plaguing her? What if he *was* her father? How would he react? Did he know about her?

As she stepped into Arthur Sinclair's path, she squared her shoulders and reminded herself that, if nothing else, he could tell her how and why he'd known her mother.

Brandon spoke. "Mr. Sinclair?"

Arthur paused and gave a polite smile. "Yes?"

"I'm Brandon De Witte and this is Juliet Blanchard. Could we have a moment of your time?" Brandon motioned him away from the throng of people milling around the front of the church building.

Arthur's quizzical gaze moved from Brandon to Juliet. He stilled. His eyes grew round, then he blinked. "Yes. Yes, of course."

Juliet gripped Brandon's hand as they moved off to the side of the church's front yard near a maple tree. Her heart beat wildly in her chest. Arthur Sinclair's astonished reaction sent goose bumps over her arms. He had to have recognized her, or at least her resemblance to her mother. That had to be why he'd looked so stunned.

Taking a deep breath, she opened her purse and pulled out the picture of Arthur and her mother and handed it to him.

He took the photo, barely glanced at it before turning his blue gaze on her. He studied her, as if he was memorizing her face. "You look just like Trudy. You have her blond hair and her cheekbones."

The soft emotion in his voice squeezed her heart. Fighting past the lump forming in her throat, she asked, "What was your relationship with my mother?"

A sad smile twisted his lips. "We knew each for a short time. Does she know you're here?"

Juliet drew in a sharp breath and squeezed Brandon's fingers. "Wh-what?"

"Does Trudy know you're following her? She was very adamant that I not contact you." His expression became earnest and sad. "You have to believe I didn't know about you until Trudy showed up a month ago."

Juliet swayed. Her mother *was* alive! Bianca was right! Brandon's arm went around her and he escorted her to a bench.

Arthur hurried beside her. "Are you sick? Is that why she needed the money? Although she said *she* was in danger."

Brandon squatted down in front of her. "Breathe, honey. Take deep breaths," he coaxed.

Juliet did as he said. "I'm okay." Her mind worked frantically to process what Arthur confirmed. "Brandon, my mother is really *alive.*" Tears filled her eyes.

Brandon looked at Arthur. "Trudy came to see you?"

Arthur took a seat beside Juliet. "Yes. She was desperate for money. She intimated that she was running for her life, but refused to let me contact the police." He shook his head. "She was very vague. But she looked very fragile, and so very beautiful. I gave her some money. She warned me not to contact any of her family. She told me…"

He paused, his expression full of regret. "She told me about you. Had I known she carried my child back then, I would have fought for her, for you. But she'd said she had to stay with her husband for the sake of her girls."

Her throat burned with the clogging emotions working their way through her system. "But she didn't stay," Juliet managed to say.

A big hole opened in her soul. Juliet wasn't really a Blanchard. Ronald wasn't her father. No wonder she'd never gained his approval or his affection.

Arthur frowned. "I had heard a rumor that Trudy died in an accident the year after I left. I grieved for her, but I didn't know about you. I went on with my life. When she showed up on my doorstep, I…needless to say, I was shocked. But surely you must have known she was alive?"

Juliet shook her head, unable to say the words.

Brandon spoke. "Juliet and her sisters were told that Trudy died over twenty years ago. Only recently have they become aware of evidence to the contrary. Thanks to you, now we know for sure Trudy is alive. You said she was running for her life. From whom?"

Arthur continued to stare at Juliet. "I'm so sorry. I feel so bad for what you are going through."

Juliet tried to smile at the compassion in his voice. She liked his kind tone and gentle manner. She forced her mind not to contemplate what life would have been like had Arthur Sinclair been a part of her life.

Arthur turned his gaze to Brandon. "I don't know who she was running from. She wouldn't say. I wish I'd been more insistent that she let me help her. My wife chastised me for going along with Trudy's request to keep the authorities out of her situation."

"Wife?" Juliet said.

He nodded, his blue eyes tender. "I married not long after I moved to California. I have two grown children."

Through the numbness invading her, Juliet felt a spurt of shock. Though why, she couldn't guess. Of course he'd be married and have a family of his own. Which meant she had two half siblings. But her sisters would always be her sisters in her heart.

Brandon pulled Juliet to her feet. "We have to get you home where you're safe from whomever didn't want us to find out about Trudy."

Shaking away the mind-freeze that momentarily gripped her, Juliet stared at him. She wanted to stay and get to know the man who'd fathered her. But her mother was in trouble. That took priority. "I have to find my mother."

She turned to Arthur, who had risen, as well. "Did she have a car?"

He shook his head. "No. She arrived by taxi. After we talked, I dropped her off at the bus station. She wouldn't tell me where she was headed." He glanced to Brandon. "She said the girls were in danger. That if it became known that—" he shifted his gaze back to Juliet, his blue eyes troubled "—if it became known that you were my daughter, you could be harmed. I didn't expect to see you."

Ignoring the wave of apprehension that swept through her, she jumped on the one fact they had to go on. "We have to check the bus station. Find out what bus she took. And then follow her."

Brandon gripped her shoulders. "What we need to do is get you to safety. We've already had two questionable incidents happen. I'm not going to keep you in the reach of danger."

Alarm darkened Arthur's eyes. "Incidents?"

Brandon quickly filled the older man in.

Arthur grasped Juliet's hand, concern for her evident in his expression. A stranger, now her father. A man who cared for her even though he'd just met her. This was all so overwhelming she didn't know what to feel. She suppressed the urge to cry.

"You have to listen to your friend. I can check the bus station and let you know what I find," Arthur said. "I'm so angry with myself for not doing more before."

"And we can hire a team of private investigators to look for her," Brandon added.

Juliet bit her lip. "Bianca already tried that. The PI ended up dead. At the time we didn't think his death was related to Mother."

Brandon's jaw went rigid. "All the more reason to get you back to Maine and your family."

"Arthur?"

A stunning woman in her midfifties approached. Her light-chestnut hair curled attractively around an oval face, accentuating her brown eyes.

Arthur gestured the woman closer. "Dora, this is Juliet."

Dora's eyebrows rose in surprise. "Trudy's Juliet?" Arthur nodded.

Dora smiled, a welcoming smile that tugged at Juliet. She clasped Juliet's hand. "Oh, my dear. What a pleasure."

The graciousness of this woman for the daughter her husband conceived with another woman humbled Juliet. "We didn't mean to cause any problems."

Dora shook her head. "You are not a problem, but a gift."

"They're searching for Trudy," Arthur interjected.

"I wish we could help." Dora gave Arthur a censuring look as she tucked her arm through his. "Why don't you come to the house and have Sunday brunch with us?"

Juliet reached for Brandon's hand, her anchor in this turbulent crisis. "I don't know if that's a good idea."

"Neither do I," Brandon agreed. "If Trudy thought that Juliet's paternity becoming public would put her in danger, it's best if we limit contact for the time being."

Arthur's eyes misted with regret. "I'm sorry we had to find each other in these circumstances. When it is safe, please say you'll come to visit. You have two half brothers who have always wanted a sister."

She, too, had longed for brothers while growing up the youngest of five girls. Now she had them. Wow! Would they even like each other? "We'll keep in touch," she promised.

Brandon produced a business card from his wallet. "You can reach us at this number."

Arthur took the card, shook hands with Brandon and then tentatively offered Juliet a hug. She went stiffly into his embrace, feeling that at any moment she would shatter into a million pieces from the many emotions careening through her. Happiness that her mother was alive, fear that her mother was in danger. Pleasure at meeting the man whose gene pool she shared and anxiety for what the future would hold once her sisters learned the truth.

They said their goodbyes and climbed back into the rental car. Juliet tried to sort through all her thoughts, but failed. They were too many and terribly confusing. Even so, one thought seared through her soul.

"My mother is alive!"

Brandon glanced at her. "Yes, so it would seem. Don't you think you should call your sisters?"

"This is news better delivered in person." She nervously twisted a strand of hair. "I have to be the one to find her. Then maybe my sisters will finally show me some respect and realize I'm as capable as they are."

"Why would you think they don't already?"

She rolled her eyes. "Please. I'm twenty-three years old and they still treat me like a baby."

"They love you."

Guilt for her uncharitable thoughts poked at her. "I know. And I love them. I'll admit I've been flighty in the past, but I'm not anymore."

"You don't think taking off like we did was flighty?"

She wrinkled her nose at him and then turned to stare out the window at the traffic on the freeway. Up ahead the sign for the airport loomed. She twisted to face him. "Could we please stay and look for my mother?"

"Juliet, we agreed the best course of action is to return to Maine where you'll be safe. Whomever your mother is running from has tried to hurt you twice. I'm not going to let anything happen to you."

He sounded as if he really cared what happened to her. A pleased sense of well-being cloaked her, soothing the unsettled emotions charged from the day's events.

"We don't know for sure that either of those incidents are related," she argued as she sat back, but deep in her gut she couldn't ignore the nagging suggestion that the attempts to harm her were somehow connected to her mother's sudden appearance. Brandon was right. She should go back home. Bringing back confirmation that Trudy was alive would go a long way to gaining the respect she craved from her sisters.

"I'm not taking any chances with your life," he stated in a tone that brooked no argument.

Her heart did a little hiccup and she slanted him a sideways glance. "I'm really glad God brought you into my life. He knew I'd need you."

A muscle in Brandon's jaw ticked. "How can you trust Him after all you've just learned?"

She cocked her head and studied him. "I'll admit when I first discovered the picture, I was pretty angry at God, but *He* didn't deceive anyone. That was human error. Human choices. I know God loves me. He sent me you."

Brandon snorted.

"He loves you, too, Brandon. You'd see that if you just let Him in."

Brandon remained silent as he brought the car to a halt in the rental car return area. Abruptly, he faced her. "Don't go thinking I'm some sort of protector sent by God. God didn't send me to you. That was my doing."

Juliet blinked, not sure what to make of his statement or the heat with which it had been delivered. She watched him get out and head inside the little box of a structure where the car-rental employees worked. As she stepped out of the car, she sent up a quick prayer, asking for guidance. She didn't understand Brandon. But she knew what her heart felt.

And what she felt scared her.

Juliet slept for most of the plane ride back to Maine. Once they touched down, she was anxious to return to the manor and hoped her father had returned, also. If not, she would call him and confront him over the phone. Anger for his deception simmered low in her belly. Ronald Blanchard would have to answer to his daughters for the lies he'd told.

Brandon took her to the factory in his car first to retrieve her car from the parking lot. The sun was just starting its descent and the overcast sky was painted with brilliant splashes of orange and pink. The sharp contrast of color to the gloomy remnants of a recent rain reminded Juliet of God's love and hope.

No matter how bleak the situation seemed, His rays of mercy and grace shone through. She wanted to share her observation with Brandon, but paused to watch him as he inspected her car inside and out.

"What? You think someone planted a bomb?" she teased.

The worry in his eyes clutched at her throat. "I just want you to be safe."

She touched his cheek. "You're sweet, you know that? I really appreciate all you've done for me."

He captured her hand and kissed the knuckles. "'All that glisters is not gold.'"

Though she recognized the quote from Shakespeare's *The Merchant of Venice,* she was confused by the regret darkening his eyes. "Brandon?"

He brusquely released her hand. "I'll follow you to the gate." He opened her car door and motioned for her to climb in. "We'll talk tomorrow."

Juliet drove home, her mind muddled with turmoil and anxiety about her life, her parents and sisters. But mostly about Brandon.

*All that glisters is not gold.*

What was he trying to tell her?

Juliet entered the kitchen of Blanchard Manor and pandemonium broke out. Andre and Marco rushed to her side with questions and concern.

The warm welcome did little to soothe her inner chaos. "Has my father returned?"

"No," Andre said at the same time that Marco shook his head.

The negative response from the two men ground frustration into her gut. As soon as she could, she would call him.

Sonya, the housekeeper, stepped into the kitchen

and her mouth gaped slightly for a moment at the sight of Juliet. Then she bustled forward, *tsk*ing and firmly took Juliet by the arm to lead her to the front parlor where all of her sisters and her aunt waited. The urge to flee gripped Juliet because she had no desire to hurt these women she loved with the news of Trudy's affair.

"You had us scared out of our minds, young lady," Miranda admonished as she engulfed her little sister in a bear hug that squeezed the breath from Juliet's lungs.

The lines of worry etched on Bianca's face as she pulled Juliet into her arms the moment Miranda released her tore at Juliet's heart. "I can't believe you took off without so much as a word."

"I'm sorry," Juliet mumbled against her sister's shoulder.

The twins, Portia and Rissa, nudged Bianca aside and embraced Juliet in a three-way hug.

"Naughty girl!" Portia exclaimed and tightened her hold.

Normally Juliet would have rolled her eyes at the chastisement, but she hung on to her sisters with love. Would their feelings for her change once they knew she wasn't really a Blanchard? The thought sent fresh anxiety coursing through her.

Finally, Juliet was forced to face her aunt. Winnie's expression was drawn and fatigue marred the delicate skin under her eyes.

"I'm sorry, Auntie. I had to go," Juliet said as she moved closer, hoping her aunt would open her arms to her.

Winnie sighed a breath of relief that transformed her face and brightened her eyes. "I'm so glad you're home."

Winnie opened her arms and Juliet sailed into her embrace. "I love you, Auntie."

Winnie stroked her hair. "I know, dear." She took Juliet by the hand and led her to the settee. The other girls gathered close. "Tell us what was so important that you would fly across the country."

Juliet's eyebrows rose. "How did you know where I'd gone?"

Winnie waved away her question. "I have my sources. So spill."

Juliet gazed at her sisters. "You all didn't have to come home because of me."

Bianca scoffed. "Of course we did. The minute Miranda called to say you had disappeared, I flew home."

"And when Aunt Winnie called looking for you, I called Rissa. She hopped the next plane out of New York," added Portia. "Even Mick has been looking for you."

Mick was Portia's fiancé and a detective with the Stoneley Police Department. He was probably the first person she should talk to tomorrow about her mother and about the incidents in California.

"I appreciate you all so much," she said, her voice wavering with emotion.

"Okay, superchick, stop stalling," Rissa chided.

Juliet grinned. "You haven't called me that since we were little."

Rissa made a rolling motion with her hand for Juliet to get on with it.

Juliet took a breath and slowly exhaled. From her purse she took out the photo she'd found in the attic. "This is why I went to California."

She handed the picture to her aunt. Winnie's eyes widened. "Where did you find this?"

"In the attic, tucked in Mother's yearbook. Did you know about this man?"

Winnie slowly nodded. "Trudy swore me to silence."

"Let me see," Bianca said and snatched the picture from Winnie. "Who is he?"

Juliet explained everything she knew. She hated seeing the hurt in her sisters' eyes when they realized their mother had been unfaithful to their father. But she hated the compassion—or pity, she couldn't tell which—in their expressions as each girl turned her gaze on her. Juliet tried not to squirm or show how tensely she waited to find out if this news would change their feelings for her.

"You're our sister regardless," Miranda stated in a no-nonsense tone.

A chorus of agreements appeased some of Juliet's turmoil. She hadn't realized how afraid she'd been that they would be glad to have a reason not to claim her as their sister. "Thank you. I needed to hear that."

Bianca put an arm around her shoulders. Juliet put her arm around Bianca's waist. "There's more."

"Of course there is. This family thrives on drama," Rissa declared.

"I've had enough drama recently, thank you very much," Portia exclaimed. She had been recently abducted by a man whom Mick had once put in prison. Mick's daughter, Kaitlyn, had been the initial kidnapping target, but when Portia fought the man, he took both of them. Thankfully, Mick was able to save them both and put their abductor back behind bars.

"This has to do with Mother," Juliet said. Her gaze stayed on Bianca. "She's alive. She went to see Arthur a month ago."

Bianca's face paled. "I knew it."

Juliet nodded. "You did. Mother told Arthur she was in danger, but wouldn't say from whom. Arthur's going to try to follow her trail there in California and Brandon's going to hire more private investigators to find her."

"I've already retained one," Bianca stated in a shaky voice. "I'll pass on this information and have him speak with Mr. Sinclair."

"Do you think she's running from Father?" Rissa asked, her brown eyes wide with anxiety.

"He's still in Europe," Portia replied.

"Then who could Mother be afraid of?" Miranda questioned.

Juliet shook her head. She wouldn't tell them what had happened to her. It would cause them more worry.

For a long moment the girls were quiet, each lost in her own thoughts. Were they all wondering the same thing as Juliet? Had their mother been sent away or had she run away?

Winnie cleared her throat. "About Brandon…" She took Juliet's hand. "Please, explain this relationship."

"Whew, that's a tall order." Juliet tried for levity but no one smiled.

She stood to pace before the fire. She needed to sort out her feelings for Brandon. She liked him, admired him and was definitely attracted to him.

But she knew her feelings went deeper, to a level that made a future without him look bleak.

She wanted to grow old with him, to see the world with him, to have children with him. She sucked in a sharp breath. But the wall he'd put up between himself and God was an obstacle she didn't know how to breach.

# ELEVEN

Even with the obstacles between them, Juliet couldn't ignore her feelings. Turning to face her sisters, she said, "I think I've fallen in love with him."

"Wow. That's unexpected, but good," Portia said with a smile. "I like him."

"So do I," Miranda stated. "He had good manners."

Bianca rose and came to Juliet. "You haven't known him long. Are you sure?"

Juliet nodded. "I've never felt like this before. I trust him."

"Trust is important. Promise me you'll take things slowly," Bianca said.

"I have no choice but to take it slowly and see where it leads." She shrugged. "I don't even know how he feels about me. I know he cares, but is it love?"

Winnie regarded her with concern. "You didn't stay with him in San Francisco, did you?"

Juliet gave her aunt a half smile. "No, Auntie. I know better than that."

Winnie's worry didn't clear. Juliet went to her. "What's the matter, Auntie?"

"I don't want you to get hurt," Winnie said as she touched Juliet's cheek.

"I'll be careful," Juliet assured her.

"I think it would be a good idea for you, for all of us, to concentrate on finding Trudy."

"I want to find out what Father knows and why he lied to us," Juliet huffed.

"Me, too," chimed in Rissa.

Winnie clutched Juliet's hand. "Don't do anything rash. If Trudy is in danger, we must proceed with caution. Let Mick and the private detectives do what they're paid to do."

"I agree," Bianca said. "We have to let the authorities do their jobs."

"This from the woman who went gallivanting off to Chicago and got trapped in a mental hospital with Leo?" Juliet quipped.

Bianca's lips twisted with a wry smile. "Not the smartest move, I admit. But luckily it turned out well." She blushed, then added, "We should all go about our lives and wait for word from Mick. I don't think any of us are safe until this mystery is solved."

"Spare me the melodrama," Rissa huffed. "I've got an early rehearsal of my play tomorrow, so I'm out of here. Portia, do you mind driving me to the airport?"

Portia linked her arm through Rissa's. "Of course not."

Rissa kissed each girl's cheek.

"I'll head to the airport with you," Bianca said. "Juliet, heed Aunt Winnie's warning. Move slowly in this relationship with Brandon. You're in a vulnerable place right now. You shouldn't be making any life-changing decisions."

"What, are you my shrink now?" Juliet teased, even as she realized the truth in Bianca's words.

Bianca tugged on Juliet's long hair. "Just a concerned big sister."

Rissa, Bianca and Portia left. Miranda gave Juliet a last hug before retiring to her room.

Juliet looked at her aunt. There were still lines of worry furrowing her aunt's brow. "Something's still bothering you, Auntie. I can tell," Juliet said.

Winnie gave her a small smile. "Unfinished business with my father."

Juliet's stomach clenched tight. It seemed they both had unfinished business with the Blanchard men.

*Idiots! I'm surrounded by idiots!*

The woman fisted her hands, her mind whirling with schemes and plans. Her contact in California had failed. She'd deal with that later. At the moment, she had to decide how to get rid of Juliet before she dug any deeper.

Unfortunately, the girl had already talked with the others. Now they, too, would have to be dealt with. But first the brat.

Crossing the darkened room to the small table, she dialed a number and waited for the line to be picked up.

"What now?"

"She returned, that's what!"

"Not my fault," the person on the other end whined.

The woman curled her lip in disgust. "No. But now you have to take care of her."

"Me? Hey, I said I'd provide you information and nothing else."

"I'll triple what I owe you." She dangled the carrot.

"Triple?"

"Yes." The woman drummed her nails on the table while her offer was being contemplated.

"Okay."

She'd had little doubt money would do the trick. Greedy idiot! "Listen carefully. I'll only say this once and it better be done right or you won't see a penny."

Brandon found his uncle seated at the computer when he returned home after making sure Juliet was safely on the Blanchard grounds.

Putting his overnight bag on the floor by the couch, Brandon hitched a hip on the side of the desk. Tate glanced at him. "Ah, the prodigal son returns."

Something dark twisted in Brandon's gut. "I'm not your son."

Tate sat back and studied his nephew. "No. You're my sister's son. The boy I raised."

"Raised to hate everything Blanchard."

Tate's eyes darkened. "They've been the bane of the Connollys' existence for decades. Howard Blanchard stole my father's company from him. Have you forgotten they are responsible for your parents' deaths?"

Brandon shook his head. "No. I remember vividly. And I *have* blamed them for the accident. But..." He stood and began to pace. Juliet's words of survivor's guilt rang through his head. He tried to dismiss the idea, but it clung to him like gum on a shoe.

"But?"

"But I can't hurt Juliet. Or any of the Blanchard women. They aren't responsible."

His uncle snorted derisively. "So you'd betray your family for one of them?"

There was an undercurrent of emotion in his uncle's voice that Brandon didn't understand. Brandon remembered how Winnie Blanchard had acted when he'd visited and at the time Brandon had wondered if she'd mistaken him for his uncle.

A suspicion clicked into place. "Do you know Winnie Blanchard?"

Tate busied himself on the computer. A red flush crept up his tanned neck. "I know her."

"She seemed to think I looked familiar when we met. I thought perhaps she saw you in me."

Tate wouldn't meet Brandon's gaze. "I wouldn't know."

Brandon's suspicions grew. "And Howard Blanchard acted very peculiar when I happened upon him in the manor, as well. He called me a Connolly."

Tate slowly turned. "You saw Howard?"

"Yes. He's an ill old man who thought I was there to hurt him. Now why would he think that?"

"Because he feels guilty for having cheated our family."

Brandon stepped closer. "He said 'you can't have my daughter.' I assume he was referring to Winnie. Why would he have said that?"

Tate's jaw tightened.

"Uncle, what are you not telling me?" Brandon pressed.

Tate stood. Harsh lines bracketed his mouth. "Don't be a fool, boy. Don't set your sights on a Blanchard girl. Howard may be old and sick, but Ronald Blanchard would never allow one of his offspring to become involved with a Connolly. The minute Ronald finds out who you really are is the minute you'll be out on your ear. You have to stick to the plan. We have to act fast, while he's still in Europe. I promised my father on his deathbed."

Brandon shook his head. "No. There's been enough destruction between our families. It has to end. I won't hurt Juliet. She's suffered enough."

"Ha! None of the Blanchards know what it is to suffer."

"You're wrong, Uncle. I've spent time with Juliet and she doesn't deserve this. I'm going to tell her everything. I can only hope she'll forgive me."

Tate moved to stand at the window. "Do what you must. But don't say I didn't warn you."

Brandon stared at his uncle. He had a sneaking hunch that something more than a deathbed promise motivated his uncle's revenge.

Brandon's own need for vengeance had waned in light of helping Juliet. He had to come clean with her. Leaving his uncle to his own thoughts, Brandon went to his room where he called Juliet and arranged to meet her at The Lighthouse restaurant. The pleased tone of her voice confirmed he was doing the right thing.

He hoped his uncle was wrong. That he wasn't playing fortune's fool.

*God loves you.*

Brandon certainly didn't feel loved. He'd felt lonely and confused for most of his life. Could he be suffering from survivor's guilt as Juliet suggested?

All he knew for sure was he had to be honest with Juliet and pray…. Could he pray? Pray that she would find it in her heart to forgive him?

Winnie climbed the stairs to her father's suite on the third floor of Blanchard Manor. She rapped lightly on the big wooden door. After a moment, Howard's nurse, Peg Henderson, opened the door. Her normally tidy uniform and perfectly coiffed brown curls were slightly mussed. Dozing on the job? It wouldn't surprise Winnie. Peg ruled the roost when it came to Howard.

"What do you need?" Peg asked, her voice raspy and impatient.

Winnie drew herself up. "I need to speak with my father."

"He's resting."

The nurse's imperious tone grated on Winnie's nerves. "This is important. Let me in," Winnie demanded.

As usual, Peg made no move to do as asked. A challenge rose in her sky-blue eyes. "I said he's resting."

Winnie blinked, her cheeks warming with anger. "You are an employee. I suggest you remember that. Move aside."

For a moment Winnie didn't think Peg would comply, but then her mouth stretched in a tight smile and she bowed her head as she stepped back and allowed Winnie to enter the chamber. Winnie decided she'd have to talk to Ronald about replacing Peg. The woman was much too controlling and disrespectful to be kept around. She hadn't been like that in the beginning. Winnie wondered what had changed.

"Why don't you go have Sonya make some tea or something," Winnie directed the nurse.

The hostility in Peg's gaze reminded Winnie of a mama bear with her cub. Obviously Miss Henderson took her job seriously. Maybe too seriously. Peg left Winnie alone with her father.

Howard lay stretched out on his four-poster mahogany bed, the down quilt pulled up high and his gray head supported by stacked pillows. Winnie pulled a high-backed, Queen Anne–style chair next to the bed. Her father's eyes fluttered for a moment. His muddied gaze took in Winnie. He frowned. "Where's sweet Peg?"

Not liking the endearment, Winnie said tightly, "She went to make tea."

"Ah." He peered at Winnie. "You need some sun. I need some sun. Help me outside, Win girl. I need to get outside." He sat up and tried to throw the covers off.

Having come to terms with her father's condition long ago, Winnie placed a gentle, restraining hand on his shoulder. "No, Father. It's blustery and cold out. There's no sun today."

He flopped back. "Killjoy. Just like *her.*"

"I'm sure Peg is doing what's best for you."

He harrumphed. "What do you want?"

"I need to talk to you." She took a deep breath. "About Tate Connolly."

Howard jerked and narrowed his eyes. "Don't speak the Connolly name in my presence."

"I *will* speak it. You and Ronald ruined my life with your meddling!"

"Bah! The Connollys are no good. I saved you from him."

"No, Father. You took the love of my life away from me with your manipulations and machinations. It wasn't right. You had no right to interfere."

Howard glared at her, hatred vivid in his now-bright gaze. "I had every right. The Connollys are backstabbing, lying vultures."

Where was this venom coming from? "I don't understand you."

The stubborn jut of his chin set her teeth on edge.

"Lester Connolly stole my Gladys!" Howard declared. His sour expression made the lines in his aged face deeper. "Gladys was mine. *Mine,* I tell you. Then Lester stole her from me. But I showed him. I took away his company, and I will make sure that no Connolly ever succeeds."

The wind left Winnie's lungs. Portia had told the girls last month that Howard had gotten worse, but

Winnie hadn't been able to accept the ugly truth. She sat back in the chair, trying to sort out the information her father had revealed. This had all started with some sordid love triangle. Howard and Lester Connolly had loved the same woman, who obviously chose Lester over Howard. Howard blamed Lester, took his company from him and then worked to keep Winnie and Tate apart. And now Juliet was in love with Brandon, Lester's grandson.

What a tangled web.

"This has got to stop. You've interfered in my life. Ronald and Trudy's lives."

Howard narrowed his eyes. "That one was a gold digger. Just wanted our money. Good thing she left the girls here where we can take care of them."

Winnie clenched her hands. "You and Ronald have to stop interfering. I won't let you two hurt the girls. You've already hurt one granddaughter and pushed her far away." Delia had moved to Hawaii and rarely came home because of Ronald and Howard.

"Too much like her grandmother, that one," he stated in a cold tone.

"Did you even love my mother?" she asked, her voice wavering slightly.

Howard gave her a sidelong glance. "Your mother?"

Winnie sat forward. "My mother, your wife, Ethel."

"Ethel." He smiled, a dreamy smile, and for a moment he was lost inside his head. "Where is Ethel? She hasn't come to see me."

Winnie closed her eyes, sadness for her father's condition filling her soul. Her mother had been dead for years. "She's gone, Father."

"Oh, right. Another woman who left me," he said with an undercurrent of bitterness.

A tear slipped down Winnie's cheek. "She died of cancer. She'd didn't leave you."

"I loved Ethel," he stated, his eyes now filled with tears.

"I'm glad to hear that, Father."

"Where's Peg?" Howard sat up again, his movements jerky, agitated. "I need my tea. Where's Peg?" He stared at Winnie, his gaze cloudy with confusion, and drew back. "Who are you? What do you want?"

Winnie narrowed her gaze. "Father?"

"I don't like it here. I want to go," Howard exclaimed as he slid out of the bed. His bare feet hit the wood floor with a thud. His flannel nightclothes hung on his gaunt frame. His distress became acute. "Help me! I'm trapped here!"

Winnie grabbed his arm as panic flared. "Father, you must lie down."

He pulled out of her grasp and stumbled sideways.

A gasp echoed in the room as Peg rushed in. She

set the tray with a pot of tea on the side table. "Howard!"

He stopped moving and reached for her. She took his arm and led him back to the bed. Turning a cold gaze on Winnie, she said, "Leave now. You shouldn't aggravate him like this. It's not good for his health."

Winnie watched as Peg soothed Howard back to a peaceful state. Winnie's heart ached for all the pain the two families had suffered because of one man's jealousy.

She had to find a way to undo the damage done between her and Tate.

A half hour later, Winnie drove her sedan to Lookout Cape, a point on the road not far from Blanchard Manor. People could park their cars in the small parking lot and walk to the stone wall built along the edge of the cliff to watch the waves of the Atlantic Ocean churn and bubble in all their magnificent glory.

Winnie was early. With the wind howling outside, she remained in her warm car and nervously twirled her earring. After leaving her father's room, she'd called Tate on his cell phone. He'd agreed to meet her here. Winnie could tell by the less than enthusiastic tone of Tate's voice that he didn't think they had anything left to say to each other. But Winnie had plenty to say.

A few minutes later, Tate arrived in a dark-green Mini Cooper. Pulling her black, wool, full-length coat tightly around her, Winnie got out of her car and met Tate on the paved sidewalk between the parking lot and the wall.

"A little cold out here, don't you think?" he said, his already ruddy cheeks quickly turning redder from the wind. He turned up the collar on his distressed brown leather bomber jacket.

She nodded and moved to the gray stone wall. Tate followed. "I love coming here on days like this," she said. She closed her eyes. "I like to feel the wind, rain and the saltwater on my face. It's very cleansing."

"Hmm."

She turned to look at him. His gray eyes regarded her with a probing query. She took a step closer to him and touched his cold cheek with her hand. "I can't believe we've found each other again."

His eyes darkened. "I've always known where you were."

She drew back. He'd known where she was, but never come for her. "I never hid."

"No, you didn't. But you didn't contact me, either."

She turned to look at the tossing waves. "No. You're right. I regret that. I regret all the years we've been apart, but I know God had a purpose. If you and I had remained together, I wouldn't have been at the manor to raise the girls."

"So there was a point to our pain?"

"Something like that. But I don't think it's too late for us to rekindle what we once had."

"Ever the optimist." He shifted to face the ocean. "My showing up now in your life was not random."

"God works in mysterious ways."

"God had nothing to do with this. I came here to destroy Blanchard Fabrics," he said harshly.

Somehow that didn't surprise her, but hurt nonetheless. "And Brandon?"

He nodded. "Yes, Brandon, too. Only he's having second thoughts because of his relationship with Juliet."

Winnie's heart lightened. "At least one romance might have a chance."

Tate scoffed. "You really think Ronald and Howard will let a relationship between them happen? There's too much bad blood between our families."

She put her hand on the sleeve of his leather jacket. "Bad blood that has nothing to do with us *or* the children." Her pulse raced as she laid bare her heart. "I want to find a way for us. A second chance at love."

He continued to stare out at the churning waves. "I channeled my frustration and anger into revenge. Especially after my father died. I swore to him I'd make Howard pay."

She tugged on his sleeve to gain his attention. When he shifted his gaze to her, she said, "Tate, my father has Alzheimer's. Nothing you could do would hurt him. It would only hurt me and the girls."

"But Ronald—"

"Is a bitter man who has alienated his children." She told him of Trudy and of the news Juliet brought back from California. "Can't you see that Ronald's own behavior has already hurt him?"

Tate seemed to be absorbing her words. She continued, "Yes, you could put Blanchard Fabrics out of business. And when that's done, what then? Will you finally be at peace, or will you start looking for someone else, something else to fill the void in your life?"

Tate scrubbed a hand over his face. "I don't know. I've hurt for so long."

The echo of bleakness in his tone stabbed at her. She could only try to direct him to the One who could comfort him. "Have you turned to God?"

His mouth pressed into a grim line. "After you left school, I couldn't seek God anymore."

Her heart ached for him. "He's always ready to listen."

Tate closed his eyes as if pained. "And you, Winnie? Are you ready to listen?"

"I'm not going anywhere," she replied, her voice steady and sure.

When he opened his eyes and gazed at her, there was a smoldering invitation in the depths of his eyes. "I never stopped loving you, Winnie Blanchard. I tried, but I couldn't."

A heavy weight she hadn't realized she carried lifted and her spirit soared over the crashing waves below. He'd never stopped loving her.

A pleading earnestness softened his features. "Can we start over? Learn who we've become?"

A smile melted over her. "That's a wonderful idea."

Tate straightened. "Would you do me the honor of accepting a dinner invitation?"

Feeling younger than she had in years, she said, "I'd love that."

He took her in his arms. "May I kiss you, Miss Blanchard?"

She clutched his shoulders. "You'd better, Mr. Connolly."

His head dipped and their lips met in a tentative, sweet kiss full of promise.

Whatever obstacles came their way, Winnie was determined not to let anything come between them a second time.

Especially not her father and brother. Never again.

# TWELVE

Standing in her walk-in closet, Juliet discarded yet another outfit onto the pile growing on the floor at her feet. Giddy anticipation ran a rapid race through her system as she tried to pick just the perfect combination of clothing for her dinner with Brandon.

He'd said he had something important to tell her. She'd held her breath as she asked if what he had to tell her had anything to do with her mother or Mr. Sinclair. He'd said no, being very cryptic. He wanted to talk about them. As a couple. Which could only mean…

Ugh! She fingered the wool duster hanging next to a glittery top. Did Brandon intend to declare his feelings? Or was he going to tell her he didn't want to pursue a relationship with her?

He cared. She knew he did. But how much? She'd promised Bianca she'd move slowly where Brandon was concerned. But she couldn't help hoping that a relationship with him could be a possibility.

Taking the duster from the hanger and slipping it on, she stared at her reflection in the mirror. She didn't look any different. She didn't feel that much different. She was still Juliet.

But who was Juliet?

A woman not really belonging to two different families.

She'd tried to gain respect and approval from her father, but now to have found out he wasn't even her father left her adrift.

A light knock sounded against the door, drawing her attention away from her musings. Juliet opened the door to Sonya.

"This was just delivered for you," the older woman said and held out a small, square envelope with her name typed on the front.

"By whom?"

Sonya shrugged. "A delivery service."

"Thank you, Sonya," Juliet said.

The housekeeper nodded and walked down the hall.

Closing the door, Juliet leaned against the wood as she opened the envelope and took out the paper. She read the typed words on the small, square sheet.

She frowned and reread the words.

Brandon is not what he seems. His attention
to you is fake. A means to an end. An end to
Blanchard Fabrics. He's using you. Use your
head. Think. You'll see I'm right. Ask him
about Connolly.

The name rang a bell. Wasn't that the name of
the man whom Grandfather had taken the factory
from? What kind of sick joke was this? Who would
send her such a thing?

Brandon had been nothing but kind and
generous to her.

Yet…a prickling of doubt crept into her mind.

He'd sought her out while she was still at school.

He'd ended up in the job her father had
promised to her.

He'd acted strangely at times. Had he been
searching her father's office for something other
than business material?

What was his connection to the Connollys?

Why had he accompanied her to California? His
own agenda? Which was what?

*All that glisters is not gold.*

She crumpled the note in her fist. It couldn't be
true. She wouldn't believe it. Brandon had supported her through one of the most traumatic times
in her life; he'd been kind and protective. There was
no way he could be using her.

Grabbing her purse, she hurried from the house

and drove to The Lighthouse restaurant as quickly as the weather conditions would allow.

Rain drizzled down her back as she rushed from the parking lot to the restaurant entrance. Inside she shivered away the cold as heat from the huge stone fireplace in the rustic dining room swirled around the patrons of the restaurant.

She spied Brandon already seated near the window where they'd have a spectacular view of the cliffs and the ocean. Any other time, she'd have appreciated the gesture, but at the moment, her thoughts were centered on the crushed note inside her purse.

Brandon rose as she approached the table. He looked handsome in his dark slacks and cream-colored sweater. His honey-blond hair was damp from the rain. He moved to hold out her chair. She nodded her gratitude for his gentlemanly manners and sat.

"You look lovely," he said once he'd resumed his own seat.

"Thank you." She took a sip of water from the goblet in front of her, giving herself a moment to gather her thoughts. She'd find out why he'd asked her here before she mentioned the note. *If* she mentioned it at all. "You said you have something important to tell me."

"I do." His gaze sought hers. "There's much I need to say. But first let's order our meal."

Food was the last thing on her mind. She pretended to look at the menu. The words swam before her eyes. Putting the menu down, she reached out to touch Brandon's hand. His skin felt warm and alive. "I need to ask you something."

He laid aside his menu, also. His earnest gaze trapped hers. She swallowed, not sure she wanted to know the answers to the questions that silly note raised. But she also knew she wouldn't be able to enjoy dinner or his company unless she proved to herself the note was some stupid prank. "Does the name Connolly mean anything to you?"

He stiffened beside her. His expression stilled and became serious. "Why do you ask?"

She hated when people answered questions with questions. "Why are you evading my question?"

He curled his fingers tightly around hers. He took a deep breath then slowly exhaled. "My mother was a Connolly."

For a moment she couldn't breathe. She tried to pull her hand away. He wouldn't let her. "You're a Connolly."

"Yes," he affirmed.

She yanked her hand away and dug out the note. Laying it on the table, she spread out the wrinkles. "Is this true? Am I just a means to an end for you?"

A muscle jumped in Brandon's jaw as he stared at the page. "I can explain."

She blinked, the world suddenly spinning.

It was true. He'd used her. Anger exploded in her

chest and spattered her with bits of sharp residue, making everything inside of her throb.

She'd fallen in love with him and he'd been using her.

"You lumpish, hasty-witted horn-beast," she muttered before abruptly rising and knocking her chair over as she stormed from the restaurant.

Bolts of panic shot through Brandon as he grabbed the offending note from the table and rushed after Juliet. He caught her in the lobby just as she was about to push open the outer door.

"Let go of me." She pulled against his hold on her elbow.

"Not until you hear me out," he said and propelled her toward the seclusion of the outside balcony. The wind whipped her hair in a frenzied dance. He led her to a corner where he could shelter her from the elements with his back.

The hurt and disappointment shining in her glare made him wince. "Juliet, listen to me. I didn't mean for you to get hurt. I never meant—"

She scoffed. "You never meant for me to find out?"

"I came here tonight to tell you."

Crossing her arms over her chest, she said, "Then tell me."

He ran a hand through his windblown hair. "I told you about my parents' accident."

Her eyes held a hint of compassion. "Yes."

"They were arguing. My mother lost control of the car."

"What does this have to do with us?" she asked slowly.

"My parents were arguing about the Blanchards."

Juliet's gaze shifted away toward the distant ocean. "Do you know why?"

"I didn't at the time, but as I grew older, I learned why."

Her gaze came back. "Because of what my grandfather did to your grandfather?"

He drew back, blinking. "You knew?"

Her mouth twisted. "We found out a few weeks ago. Grandfather confessed to Portia."

"Then you understand how I had grown to hate your family. I wanted revenge for the wrongs that had been done."

"Oh, yeah. I understand. You're just like him. My grandfather used underhanded means to get what he wanted. And so did you. You used me."

Guilt wagged a finger at him. "Yes. At first. I admit that I sought you out to gain information about your family. My plan backfired because I was falling in love with you. With your creativity and your spirit. I thought you were on your way to a career away from Stoneley. I was honestly as surprised as you when you showed up at the office."

"But you knew you'd be there," she countered. "All along you've been working to…what? To find some way to ruin my family?"

Shame withered in his soul. "Yes. I wanted vengeance."

She shook her head, a sad light reflecting in her green eyes. "Vengeance is God's, not yours. He decides who's punished and who's not. You had no right to use me like this. No right to make me think there was something between us."

His heart squeezed tight. "But there is, Juliet. That's what I wanted to tell you tonight. I'd planned to come clean and ask for your forgiveness."

"Why should I believe you?" She pushed past him. "I don't think I can believe anything you say anymore."

"Juliet, please don't go."

Turning slowly to face him, her expression hard, bitter, she said, "I never want to see you again."

His heart bled as she walked away. Who cared about vengeance? He might have lost his chance at love.

Numb from shock, Juliet drove back to the manor. She let the tears fall down her cheeks but she barely felt their hot trails. It seemed her whole being had turned to stone. She was cold. So cold. Her heart felt brittle and fragile. At any moment it would shatter and she'd be left with nothing inside, just a hollow cavity.

How could Brandon have done this? Why hadn't she been aware of his agenda? She'd been so blind, accepting him at face value. Drinking up his care and concern and letting her heart open to him.

She pulled into the garage, turned off the motor and let the night air seep into her already-iced veins.

"Lord, why? Why do I hurt? Why did I fall in love with him?"

Every man in her life had betrayed her in one way or another.

Feet heavy with the burden of hurt weighing her down, Juliet left her car and went inside. The warmth of the kitchen stung. She wasn't sure if feeling the pain was a good sign or not.

"Miss Juliet," Marco said as he entered the kitchen from the hallway that led to the employees' rooms. "You missed dinner. Only Miss Miranda was here to eat. Can I make you a plate?"

"No." She waved him away as she shuffled across the tile floor.

"Are you okay? Do I see tears?"

She wiped at the moisture still leaking from her eyes. "I'm…" What? Fine? Hardly.

"I know what you need. My special brownies. I'll have some brought to your room."

Not really caring one way or the other, she shrugged. "Thanks."

She slogged through the house to her room and

threw herself onto the bed. Thankfully, she hadn't encountered her sister or her aunt. She couldn't face either at the moment. How was she going to tell her family about Brandon's duplicity?

She could just imagine the way Bianca would give her that look that said, "I'd thought better of you."

No wonder they all still treated her like a child. She had horrible judgment.

A knock on the door drew her to her feet. She opened the door and found Sonya with a plate of thick chocolate squares complete with chocolate frosting.

"Marco said you were upset. Can I help?" Sonya stepped closer and softened her voice. "The affairs of the heart are hard at times."

Juliet raised her eyebrows. "How did you—"

"I heard you tell your sisters you are in love. I can guess the young man has brought on these tears."

"Yes. Well. I don't plan to shed any more on his behalf." Reaching for the plate of brownies, Juliet stated, "Nothing an overdose of chocolate can't cure."

Sonya gave her a motherly smile. "Don't eat so many you get sick."

Giving the older woman a quick smile, Juliet replied, "I won't."

Once Sonya retreated, Juliet sat on her bed and

dived into the brownies. The lush confection practically melted in her mouth. If only the chocolate could melt away the ache in her heart.

Would Brandon have the gall to show up at the office the next morning? How would she deal with him if he did?

When Ronald found out, he was going to be livid. Not that she cared what Ronald felt at this point. He'd lied to his children. He'd told them their mother was dead.

Did he know about Arthur Sinclair? She figured he probably did. Could that have been why her mother had gone away? Not because of the postpartum depression, as they'd been told?

Did Ronald know what his father had done to the Connollys? Probably. How did he feel about it?

So much deceit.

Feeling sorry for herself wasn't helping. Her head pounded behind her eyes. Her heart picked up speed. She set the brownies aside, suddenly nauseous. Great! On top of everything she'd eaten too many of the rich sweets.

Her stomach spasmed. She gasped and clutched at her middle. Her heart felt as if it would rip through her chest with the force of its beat. The pain in her abdomen grew. With a moan, she stood. The room whirled.

She reached out a hand to grab something, anything that would steady her. Her hand found only air. The world spun in a crazy spiral as she toppled to the floor. She closed her eyes and let the darkness take her.

When Brandon returned to his condo, his uncle was not there. Feeling lonely and heartsick, Brandon sat in the dark on the couch. He'd never meant to hurt Juliet. She deserved so much more, had been through so much as it was, that he was a complete heel to have used her. His motives had been so wrong and distorted. He wanted to cling to the anger and need for revenge that had driven him for so long, but there was nothing but grief in his soul from losing Juliet. He realized with sharp clarity that he loved her and wanted to spend the rest of his days cherishing her.

He hoped one day she'd find it within herself to forgive him. To let him close again. Maybe love him as he loved her.

A taunting inner voice jeered at him, saying he didn't deserve a second chance. He knew he didn't but that didn't keep him from hoping.

The quiet of the room was shattered by the ringing of the phone. He picked up the receiver. "Yes."

"Little Miss Blanchard didn't like hearing about your hidden agenda." A disembodied voice cackled with glee. "Well, if you value your girlfriend's life, you'll convince her to stop looking for her mother.

Or she won't be walking away from you again. She won't be able to walk at all. Because she'll be dead. In her own bed!"

Brandon jerked as if struck. "What? Who is this?"

The caller hung up.

His blood pounding in his ears, Brandon called the Blanchard house. The housekeeper acknowledged that Juliet was home but refused to put her on the line. He hung up in the middle of the woman's scolding for making Juliet cry.

Grabbing his keys, he bolted out the door. Juliet was in trouble. He could only hope she'd let him protect her.

He broke the speed limit across Stoneley and skidded to a halt at the big iron gate. He got out of his car and laid on the buzzer.

A few moments later a woman's voice came through the intercom box. "Yes?"

"This is Brandon De Witte. I need to see Juliet."

"I told you she's resting."

"Let me in, now!" Brandon barked. "She's in danger!"

There was a moment of silence before the big iron gate began to open, the hinges squeaking in protest. Brandon jumped back in his car and sped up the long drive to the house. He killed the engine, hopped out and rang the bell.

The door was opened by a middle-aged woman he remembered as the housekeeper. She glared at him. "Stay put. I will see if Miss Juliet will see you," she said as she closed the door behind him.

Without waiting for a reply, she turned on her heel and headed up the stairs. Brandon paced the entryway, his soft-soled shoes making a squishing noise as he went. The fragrance from the large bouquet of colorful flowers on the round table in the center of the foyer burned his sinuses.

He ran a hand through his hair. He hoped Juliet wouldn't refuse to see him. He needed to know she was okay. He had to make her see how important it was that she contact the police now.

A scream splintered the air.

# THIRTEEN

Brandon tore up the stairs and turned down the hall in the direction that Sonya had disappeared. At the far end a door stood open. He rushed inside and found Sonya bent over an unconscious Juliet.

His heart lurched as he knelt beside Juliet. He checked her pulse. She was alive. Barely. Clawing panic ripped at him and he shuddered. *Oh, God, please don't let her die!*

He couldn't take losing another person that he loved.

"What happened? I heard a scream," Miranda said as she entered the room. Her eyes grew round at the sight of Juliet. She looked as if she might faint. "Is she…"

Brandon scooped Juliet up and stood. "She's alive. But I have to get her to a hospital."

"I'll call an ambulance." Sonya bustled toward the door.

Hurrying past Miranda, Brandon followed

Sonya down the stairs. "An ambulance will take too long. I'll drive her."

Miranda followed at his heels. "Maybe Grand-father's nurse, Peg, should examine her."

"No time. She needs more care than she can get here," Brandon replied. He yanked open the front door and rushed out to his car. Miranda stood on the stairs, her hands clutched at her throat.

Brandon laid Juliet across the backseat of his car. "Come on, honey. You hang in there."

He left the Blanchard estate on squealing tires and sped toward the Stoneley Hospital. The seven-minute drive seemed as though it took hours. Fear roiled in his gut. What would he do if he lost her? He screeched to a halt at the emergency room entrance and jumped out of the car.

"Hey, you can't park there," a security officer called out.

"I need some help here," Brandon yelled back as he opened the back door and gently pulled Juliet out. The officer ran inside and returned with an orderly and a gurney. Together they secured Juliet's unconscious form on the stretcher before the orderly whisked her inside.

"Can you take care of the car?"

The guard nodded.

Brandon tossed his keys to the security guard, then dogged the orderly's footsteps.

A nurse intervened at the double metal doors

leading to the emergency exam room. "Sir, you can't come back here."

"Is she going to be okay?" he asked, trying to see through the doors. He hated leaving Juliet's side.

"We'll do our best. Are you her husband?"

He glanced at the older woman in green scrubs. His heart twisted. "No. Friend." But he wanted to be so much more.

"You'll need to wait over there, sir." She directed him to the waiting area.

Brandon couldn't sit. His heart pumped and his thoughts raced. What had happened to Juliet? Did her collapse have to do with the other threats on her life? Or had the mysterious caller made good on his threat so quickly?

Brandon used his cell phone to call the manor and let Miranda know they'd made it safely and Juliet was being cared for.

"I'll call the others," she promised before hanging up.

Next Brandon called the local police department.

"I need to speak to someone about some threats made on Juliet Blanchard's life," he told the man who had answered the phone at the station.

"One moment."

Brandon rocked on his heels as frustration pulsed through his veins. He should have done this straightaway when they returned from California, but he'd been too engrossed in his feelings for Juliet to think clearly.

A voice crackled over the line. "This is Detective Mick Campbell."

"Detective, Juliet Blanchard's life is in danger. She's at the hospital now. She needs some protection."

"And you are?"

"Brandon De Witte. We're at Stoneley Hospital now."

"I'm on my way. Do not leave." The line disconnected.

Brandon hung up. He wasn't going anywhere until Juliet was safe.

Thirty minutes later, Brandon still paced the linoleum floor of the waiting area. People bustled about—nurses, doctors and other staff. A few other people sat in the hard-backed chairs waiting for word of their loved ones. Brandon had never felt more alone or more scared in his adult life.

"De Witte?"

Brandon turned to find two men approaching. Both were tall with short-cropped hair and intense stares. One lean, the other brawny. "I'm Brandon De Witte."

"Detective Mick Campbell," the brawny one said. "This is my partner, Detective Drew Lancaster."

They shook hands, each warily assessing the other.

"So, you say Miss Blanchard is in some kind of

danger?" Lancaster asked as he crossed his arms over his chest, his off-the-rack beige sport coat pulling at his shoulders.

Brandon told them of the events in California, the phone call and of finding Juliet unconscious in her bedroom.

"I'll go see the status of the victim," Lancaster said and moved toward the administration desk.

"What's your relationship with Juliet?" Campbell queried.

"We're friends," Brandon answered, aware of Campbell's perceptive blue eyes studying him.

"How is it you were in California with her?" He took a notepad and pen out of the breast pocket of the leather jacket he wore.

Not about to reveal Juliet's private life, he said, "We went on business. I work at Blanchard Fabrics with Juliet."

"How long have you worked there?"

Brandon frowned. "Less than a month."

"Did you report these incidents in California to the authorities?"

"No, but I'm reporting them now."

"Did you get a license number for the car that ran you off the road?"

Brandon shook his head. "No. It happened too fast."

Campbell's mouth tightened. "Tell me about tonight. Start with the phone call."

Brandon again retold the threats the mysterious voice had made on the phone and about rushing to Blanchard Manor to warn Juliet.

"Did you try to call the manor first?"

"Yes. But the housekeeper wouldn't let me talk with Juliet."

"Why not tell Sonya that Juliet might be in trouble?"

"Sonya was too busy yelling at me to get a word in."

The detective eyed him. "Why was she yelling at you?"

Heat climbed up Brandon's neck. "Because earlier Juliet and I had a...we argued. And she was crying."

"What was the argument about?"

"It was personal."

Campbell made a note. "So you drove to Blanchard Manor."

"The housekeeper went to see if Juliet would speak with me. I heard a scream, I ran up the stairs and found Juliet lying unconscious on the floor of her room."

"What was Sonya doing when you entered the room?"

"Crying. Trying to wake Juliet up."

"Who else was home?"

"Miranda. I don't know who else."

"Why didn't you wait for the ambulance?"

Brandon ran a hand through his hair. "It was faster to bring her myself."

Campbell contemplated him a moment. "What is your relationship with Juliet?"

"I've already told you. We work together."

"Right." Campbell made another note on his pad. "But you argued and she cried."

"Mick!"

Detective Campbell spun around as Miranda and one of the twins moved down the hall toward where the two men stood. Miranda walked at a sedate pace, her complexion leached of color and her eyes dark with worry.

The other sister rushed forward. Her dark curls were captured at the nape of her neck with a scarf and her big, dark eyes were trained on the detective.

Campbell caught her as she threw herself against him. "Easy now, Portia."

She buried her face in his chest for a moment, her body shuddering. When she lifted her head, tears streaked down her pale cheeks. "Where is she? Is she all right?" Portia turned her gaze on Brandon. "Brandon? What happened?"

"You know each other?" Campbell asked.

Portia nodded. "He's Juliet's boss and...well, yeah."

Detective Lancaster came back. "They've taken her to ICU."

Portia gasped. "I need to see her."

Lancaster looked pointedly at Campbell. "We need to talk."

Campbell held Portia's hands. "Call your other sisters and your aunt. Do you have your cell phone with you?"

Portia nodded as more tears slipped down her cheek.

Campbell wiped a tear with his finger and dropped a kiss on her forehead. "We'll get through this."

She gave him a watery smile.

He released her hands and turned his probing eyes on Brandon. "Stay put."

"I'm not going anywhere," Brandon assured him.

The two detectives walked away.

Miranda moved close and put an arm around Portia's slim shoulders. "This is horrible."

Portia touched Brandon's arm. "Tell us what happened."

He told them about the threatening phone call and of finding Juliet unconscious in her room.

Portia led Miranda to a chair and then moved away to make her calls. Brandon resumed pacing like a caged animal. He had to do something, find some way to help Juliet. His heart ached with the need to see her, to touch her. To tell her he loved her and beg her not to walk away.

Needing more space than the small waiting room offered, he walked down the hall away from where Portia talked on the phone. He asked a passing nurse where the ICU unit was located.

Taking the elevator, he arrived at the fourth floor and was told he could wait in the chapel if he wanted, but he couldn't enter the Intensive Care Unit.

Brandon stared at the dark-paneled wooden doors of the hospital chapel.

Juliet believed God loved her. She'd even claimed God loved Brandon. Her faith was such a rock for her. She needed that faith now. Brandon moved forward and entered the quiet sanctuary. The faint scent of lemon polish teased his nose. Gleaming wood and radiant stained-glass artwork set off by low lighting gave the chapel a tranquil and soothing ambience.

He sat on a pew near the front. He wasn't sure what to do or say, so he just sat quietly with his eyes closed. Worry for Juliet gnawed at him, making him restless. He tried to calm his mind, to let the stillness of the small chapel infuse him with some peace.

Images flipped through his consciousness, like a movie projector gone haywire. Juliet's face as she'd said she never wanted to see him again. The conviction in Juliet's eyes as she talked of God's love.

The images came faster now. Going back in time to days when his parents were alive. His mother's smile. His father on his knees praying.

*God is always faithful, Brandon,* his father had once said.

Juliet's voice whispered in his memory. *God protected you. He has a plan for you.*

"God, if You're really there, Juliet needs You now," he said aloud, his voice echoing softly in the silent room. "I need You."

He buried his face in his hands. "I need *her.*"

"What if it's something bad?" Winnie fretted as she and Tate rode the elevator to the hospital's fourth floor. When Portia had called with the news that Juliet had collapsed, Tate had immediately insisted on driving Winnie to the hospital.

Tate took Winnie's hand in his. "We have to hope for the best."

Touched that he was able for the moment to put aside his personal grudge against her family and show compassion for her niece, Winnie drew in a breath. "I should have been at the house."

Tate squeezed her hand. "You couldn't have stopped whatever happened."

She knew that, but she hated feeling so helpless. One of her girls was hurt. She loved them as if they were her own and she'd do anything for each and every one.

The elevator doors slid open. Winnie and Tate stepped out and saw Miranda, Portia, Mick and another man standing at the far end of the hall. Winnie picked up the pace and Tate let go of her hand. She noted that he hung back, but she stayed focused on her niece. "Girls, Mick. When can I see Juliet?"

"The doctors are still working on her. They'll come out when she's stable enough for visitors," Miranda replied.

That didn't sound good. "What happened?"

Portia hung on to Winnie at the waist. "They pumped her stomach and gave her charcoal. Aunt Winnie, they think she was poisoned!"

"Oh, no!" For a moment Winnie clung to Portia until the sensation of dizziness passed. "Who would do such a thing?"

Mick and the other man, whom Winnie now remembered as Detective Lancaster, exchanged a glance.

Mick said, "We haven't uncovered the source. But we have reason to believe that someone wants to do Juliet harm because of at least two other unconfirmed attempts on her life."

Miranda's gasp echoed Winnie's.

Portia's voice quaked. "We didn't know. She never said anything. How can this be?"

Detective Lancaster asked, "Do you know of anyone who would want to hurt Juliet?"

All three women shook their heads.

Winnie pinned Mick with her gaze. "Do you think it has anything to do with the girls' search for their mother?"

He inclined his head. "It could. Have Bianca and Rissa been notified?"

Portia nodded. "Yes. They're both on their way. I also left a message for Delia. Seems she's on another island at the moment."

Mick held Portia's gaze, affection and understanding shining in the blue depths. "Remember, God's in control."

Portia clung to him for a moment.

Winnie watched the interplay between the two and smiled. After all that they'd gone through with the kidnapping of Mick's daughter and Portia, she was thankful to see their relationship so solid and built on the foundation of God's love.

Winnie glanced around and found Tate standing near the nurses' station, leaning against the wall. She didn't want him to feel left out; she tried to say as much with her expression. He dipped his chin slightly and smiled in understanding.

Winnie returned her attention to Mick. "What kind of poison?"

Lancaster answered. "The doctor said there was a high level of glycoside in her blood work."

Portia asked, "Which is?"

"A substance found in heart medications," replied the detective. "Did Juliet have a heart condition?"

"No," Winnie answered.

"Does anyone in the house have a heart condition? Howard, maybe?" Mick asked.

The women looked at each other. Miranda spoke up, "We don't think so. You should ask Grandfather's nurse. She would know."

Mick nodded and looked to Lancaster. "We should go to the house."

Lancaster nodded. "I had a unit secure the premises and called forensics. We'll meet them there."

"I'll come with you," Portia said.

Mick's gaze was tender on Portia. "Shouldn't you stay here?"

Indecision played across Portia's face. "I have to know what happened to Juliet."

Thinking it would be easier on the staff to have a Blanchard there to grant the police access to the house, Winnie touched Portia's arm. "I'll call you if anything changes here."

Portia gave Winnie and Miranda a quick hug before leaving with Mick and his partner.

"Miranda, would you be a dear and find me a cup of coffee? I have a feeling it's going to be a long night."

Miranda blinked and looked past her aunt toward the long hall. Then she squared her shoulders. "Of course, Aunt Winnie."

Winnie watched her niece walk away. It was

good to see Miranda out of the house, but the circumstances were appalling. Why would someone want to hurt Juliet?

As soon as Miranda was out of sight, Winnie hurried to Tate and filled him in.

"My dear, I'm so sorry." Tate took her hands. "What can I do?"

"I don't know." Anxiety gnawed at her. "I need to pray. Would you join me?"

Tate looked toward the chapel doors at the end of the hall. "I'd rather not."

Her heart sank. There had been a time when Tate's faith had been as strong as her own. She blamed her father and brother for not only separating her from Tate but for separating Tate from God. At the moment she couldn't reach out to Tate. She needed to reach out to God and find comfort while Juliet lay unconscious. Tears stung her eyes. "I have to."

Tate nodded. "I'll be here."

After a parting squeeze to his hand, she went to the chapel.

# FOURTEEN

Brandon raised his arms out in a gesture of entreaty. He didn't know what more to do, how else to pray. Thinking that somehow Juliet was being punished for his sins, he cried out, "Please forgive me. Don't take out Your anger on Juliet. She doesn't deserve it. Help me, Lord, to let go of the past and live for You."

Brandon dropped his arms to his side. The ache in his head was overshadowed by the heartsick worry tightening his chest. A whisper of movement made him twist around. Juliet's aunt Winnie walked down the aisle. "Miss Blanchard?" His heart stalled. "Juliet?"

Winnie shook her head as she glided forward. "No news yet."

Thankful that no news wasn't bad news, Brandon turned to stare at the stained-glass window at the front of the small chapel. The brilliant colors, lit by tiny, well-placed bulbs, sparkled. But the beauty of the craftsmanship blurred in his vision.

Winnie sat beside him. She folded her hands and bowed her head. Brandon felt awkward, yet comforted to know another person was actively praying for Juliet.

After a moment, Winnie lifted her gaze to the cross. "God doesn't punish those who are innocent. He corrects those He loves when they've strayed from His will." She shifted to face Brandon. "You can't blame yourself for what has happened. Nothing you have done brought this on. And you can't blame God, either. There is evil in this world. That's a sorry fact."

"You don't know what I've done," Brandon said, feeling the weight of recrimination pounding on his shoulders.

Winnie covered his hand with hers, the pressure warm and sincere. "Yes, I do. Your uncle told me."

Brandon drew back. "You talked with my uncle?"

Winnie gave a soft smile and her cheeks reddened slightly. "Yes. Tate and I have a history. And hopefully a future. But he, as well as you, must see that continuing the destructive path you've been on will only lead to more destruction."

He ran a hand through his hair. "But how can we change what's already been done?"

"Forgiveness. Love. These are the antidotes to your anger and bitterness. Only through forgiveness will your heart heal and be open to love."

His head knew the truth of his heart. "I do love. I love Juliet," he stated firmly. "But she will never forgive me for what I've done."

Winnie stood. "If you really love her and can forgive our family for the wrongs done to your family, then you must fight for Juliet. Fight for your love."

Brandon stood, a renewed sense of purpose growing in his chest. He would do anything to convince Juliet, show her that his love was true. No matter how long it took.

Brandon escorted Winnie out of the chapel. He wasn't surprised to see Tate rise off a chair in the waiting room and stride toward them.

"Uncle, Miss Blanchard tells me you two have a history," Brandon said, confirming what he'd suspected earlier.

Tate gave him a rueful smile. "Yes. We do."

Winnie linked her arm through Tate's. "Has Miranda returned?"

He nodded. "Yes. She's in with Juliet. The doctor said that now we wait to see if she awakens."

Winnie gave a small gasp. "I must see her. Both of you come with me."

Brandon gladly accepted the invitation.

Tate hung back. "I'll stay here and direct any of the others to you."

Brandon could sense Winnie's disappointment. Tate wasn't so accepting of a place in Winnie's life that meant being a part of the rest of the Blanchards' lives. At a more opportune time, Brandon would share with his uncle the lessons he'd learned from the Blanchard women, but right now, his focus was on seeing Juliet.

They entered the private room Juliet had been moved to. Brandon's heart fell to his toes. Juliet lay flat in the bed, her beautiful face pale, and tubes stuck out of her nose, mouth and arms. Machines beeped softly, thankfully showing signs of life that weren't visible to the eye. It was all he could do not to rush to her and gather her into his arms and plead for her to wake up.

Miranda sat beside Juliet, her complexion pasty and her brown eyes teary. Attempting to maintain control, Brandon hung back as Winnie went to join Miranda. Seeing a few more chairs in the corner, Brandon pulled one over for Winnie. She smiled gratefully as she sat. He took a seat a little ways away. He'd give the ladies their time with Juliet, because he had no intention of leaving.

Not without his Juliet.

For two days, Brandon kept a bedside vigil over Juliet, thanks to Winnie's insistence that he be allowed to stay. Rissa and Bianca both had arrived that first evening. They were the most vocal in demanding that the doctors do more for their sister. But the doctors remained firm in their conclusion that they'd done everything medically possible and now her recovery rested in God's hands.

The police had determined that the poison Juliet had ingested had come from ground-up pieces of a poisonous plant put into the brownies she'd eaten before her collapse and not from any of Howard Blanchard's medications. Apparently, the oleander from the floral arrangement in the entryway was quite deadly.

The chef's assistant, Marco, had disappeared, making him the obvious suspect, and a statewide manhunt was now in progress. Until they found him, the "why" would remain a mystery. Because of the threatening phone call, Brandon was sure Juliet's poisoning had something to do with her search for her mother and the information she uncovered about her biological father. But how Marco played into this mess was anybody's guess.

The Blanchard women had come to visit Juliet in shifts, each spending hours holding her hand, praying and singing to her. The haunting melody that Miranda would hum played constantly at the back of Brandon's mind. He would have to ask Miranda about the tune one day.

Barbara, Ronald's assistant, had stopped by many times, as well. She assured the girls that their father was on his way home.

Brandon shifted in the small, uncomfortable chair next to Juliet's bed. For the moment he was alone with her. Portia had taken a break to grab some coffee.

He really should go home and change clothes, but he couldn't risk something happening to Juliet. He didn't tell anyone that he feared whoever had tried to hurt her would try again. The threat he'd received on the phone echoed in his brain.

The police had a guard at the door, but still, Brandon wouldn't rest until Juliet woke up. The longer she remained unconscious, the less hopeful the doctors were. But Brandon refused to think that Juliet wouldn't wake up.

She had to. He couldn't even think about life without her.

His chest hurt with impotent rage at whoever had done this to Juliet.

With a shaky touch, he stroked her hand. "It's not as gloomy today," he said. He didn't know if she could hear him, but he figured talking to her was better than the silence. "Your aunt will be here shortly. You wouldn't believe it, but she and my uncle are spending a lot of time together. Did you know they met in school in Switzerland? I never would have guessed. But then again, I never asked."

Brandon stretched out his legs, relieving some of the stiffness in his limbs. If only he could ease the ache in his heart as easily. "I called Arthur Sinclair and he sent flowers. To keep the trauma to a minimum, we thought it best for him not to come.

He's still working on following your mom's trail. But no luck yet."

He squeezed her hand. "You have to get better so when we find her you can see her."

Tears gathered at the corners of his eyes. "I love you, Juliet. No matter what happens. I'll always love you. Please come back to me. You can yell at me. You can call me a horn-beast all you want, if you'd just wake up. I promise you, Juliet, I'm not giving up on you. Never."

He leaned forward and touched his lips to the back of her hand then turned her palm up. Gently he laid his cheek against her cool skin and began to hum Miranda's haunting melody.

Juliet became aware of several things at once. She was lying flat on her back, she ached all over, something warm and heavy rested in her right hand and a deep voice hummed a tune that was familiar and left her feeling vaguely uneasy and yet comforted at the same time.

She realized the melody was something Miranda hummed when she was upset. But that wasn't Miranda's voice she heard.

Her heart whispered a name.

*Brandon.*

She sighed. The pressure in her hand lifted.

"Juliet?"

His voice. He was here with her. She wanted to

go to him. She wanted to leave the dark emptiness that clung to her. She tried to fight it. Tried to open her eyes, to speak. Nothing wanted to work. Frustration clogged her throat.

*Brandon!* her mind screamed. *Help me!*

Images flashed across her mind. Brandon's smile. The anguish on his face as he talked of his parents. His comforting presence when she'd faced Arthur Sinclair and the truth about her mother. The agony in his eyes the last time she'd seen him.

Then it all came flooding back.

He'd used her. He'd wanted to destroy her family.

She let herself sink back to the dark place.

"Your sisters will return soon. They're very worried."

Her sisters. She loved her sisters.

"Juliet, listen to me. Please, come back. We need you. I need you," Brandon said, his voice breaking.

*No!* she wanted to yell. *You just want to use me.*

The edges of her consciousness faded. She was slipping again. She wanted to sink away, but something kept her from going.

"Oh, please, God, please bring her out of this," he said, the pleading in his voice marred by emotion.

Her heart jolted; awareness zinged through her body. Brandon was praying? She struggled again to come to the surface. Her eyes fluttered. Light made her wince.

"Yes! Oh, thank You, Lord!"

Brandon's excited voice touched her. Suddenly there were other voices surrounding her and people poking at her. Someone lifted one of her eyelids; the light flooded in, making spots dance in her vision. She moaned. Something cool was placed against her lips. Water trickled into her mouth. It felt so good.

Her eyes adjusted as they opened fully. A man in a white coat smiled at her. He had kind green eyes. A nurse put a sponge to her lips again. Juliet's gaze searched past the doctor and found Brandon hovering at the foot of the bed. He looked awful. He needed a shave, his designer clothes were wrinkled and there were dark circles under his eyes. Why was he here?

"We're glad you're awake," the doctor said.

She opened her mouth and tried to speak. She coughed. The nurse lifted her torso up slightly.

"Water," she croaked.

The nurse held a cup to her lips. She drank greedily.

"Slowly," the nurse said.

"Your vital signs are good," the doctor said. "Your family will sure be glad to see you."

The doctor and the nurse left. Brandon stepped closer.

"Why are you here?" she asked, trying hard to ignore the painful squeeze of her heart and the need to ask for him to take her in his arms.

"Because I love you."

Her breath hitched. She turned her head away. Words meant nothing to him. He'd betrayed her trust, used her to gain better access to her family. She couldn't believe him.

"Please, don't turn away from me." He lifted her hand and kissed her knuckles. "You are still in danger, Juliet. Don't forget that," he said quickly as a commotion in the hall moved closer to the room. He stepped away.

"Juliet!"

Her name echoed in stereo as four of her five sisters swarmed in. Each took a turn hugging her, though mindful of her IVs. Through her laughter and tears, she saw Brandon slip out the door just as Ronald stepped in. She was surprised by his presence. Had he come home because of her? Or did he simply possess good timing?

She wasn't ready to deal with him. She closed her eyes and sank into the pillows. Bianca held her hand.

"You sure gave us a scare," Portia said from the other side of the bed.

Juliet found a smile. "I didn't mean to."

"Of course you didn't, dear," Aunt Winnie said.

Juliet opened her eyes. Winnie and Ronald stood together at the foot of the bed. How could two siblings be so different? Winnie was gracious and affectionate while her brother was terse and distant.

Bianca squeezed her hand. "Did you see Brandon?"

Juliet nodded.

"He stayed here 24-7 since you were admitted," Rissa interjected.

A melting tenderness cascaded over her heart like salve on an open wound.

"He certainly did," agreed Miranda. "He wouldn't leave except to grab a bite to eat and even then, was so quick I'm sure his food gave him indigestion."

That teased a smile from Juliet. Could she hope that his feelings were genuine? Or was all this for show? Surely he wouldn't continue with his plan now.

Ronald stepped forward, crowding Bianca to the side. "I came back as soon as Barbara called."

Juliet stared at the man she had once called Father. She didn't know what to call him now.

He sat in the chair by the bed and took her hand. "If anything were to happen… I love you, Juliet. I'm so thankful you're safe." Tears gathered in his eyes.

Juliet blinked back tears of her own. Then they were all crying and telling her how much they loved her.

"That's all I've ever wanted. Your love and respect," Juliet managed to say.

Ronald hugged her. She cried harder.

Easing away, Ronald cleared his throat. "I vow, whoever did this will pay."

Bianca and Juliet exchanged a glance rife with meaning. Now was not the time to bring up Trudy or Arthur Sinclair. Who knew how Ronald would take it. The other girls seemed to understand and they made plans for Juliet to come home.

The doctors insisted on a few days of observation, which went by quickly. Though she'd been in a coma, she'd need to sleep and regain her physical strength. Mick had kept a guard at her door. Her sisters came often but she had made sure the staff knew she didn't want to see Brandon. She wasn't emotionally ready to see him.

On the day she was released to her family's care there was a break in the storm clouds. For a moment, as she'd transitioned to the waiting Town Car, Juliet closed her eyes and turned her face to the sun peeking through the gray clouds. Her heart wanted to believe it was God's way of saying hello.

That evening, as they all gathered in the living room, Juliet knew the time to confront her father was at hand. From her place on the settee; Juliet cleared her throat, drawing everyone's attention. Bianca sat next to her on the settee, Miranda and Aunt Winnie sat across from them on the other small couch. Rissa paced in front of the fireplace and Portia sat in a plush leather chair. Their father stood by the window, staring out at the darkening sky.

"Father," Juliet said. He turned and she captured his gaze. "We have a question for you."

He arched an eyebrow. "Yes?"

Juliet cast her gaze over her sisters. Winnie gave her an encouraging nod. Bianca took her hand. Juliet knew her sister would gladly be the one to step up and demand answers, but to come to terms with her past this was something Juliet had to do. The time for answers had come.

Squeezing Bianca's hand, Juliet said, "We know Mother is alive."

"Excuse me?" A muscle ticked in Ronald's jaw. "What nonsense is this? Have you *all* gone mad?"

"No, Father," Juliet replied. "She's alive. Why did you tell us she wasn't?"

"I don't know what you're talking about."

Bianca scoffed.

Rissa stopped her pacing. "Yes, you do. You've known all along."

Ronald's glare zeroed in on Bianca. "You did this. You stirred this entire mess and wouldn't let it die."

Bianca met his glare with one of her own. "It's over, Father. I was right. You denied it then. You can't now."

"Why did you send her away?" Portia asked.

"I didn't send her away," he countered, his face turning red.

Miranda asked in her soft, firm voice, "Then why did she leave?"

Bianca stood up. "And why did you tell everyone she was dead!"

Clearly flustered, Ronald frowned. "You don't understand."

"I suggest you tell them," Winnie said, her voice hard.

Ronald's gaze darted to each girl. Juliet thought for a moment he'd continue to deny what they'd come to learn as truth, but then his resolve seemed to crumble. His shoulders drooped slightly and he ran a hand over his jaw.

"I never wanted you girls to know that your mother was mentally unstable."

Bianca fisted her hands. "Is that why you had her committed to the Westside Medical Retreat in Chicago?"

"No!" Ronald waved a hand in the air. "I knew nothing about her being institutionalized. That must have happened after she left us."

"You're still saying she left on her own?" Portia asked, her dark eyes doubtful.

"She was unbalanced. I was afraid for you girls."

Rissa spun away from him and stared into the flames of the fire. "So that justifies faking her death?"

"I wanted to spare you girls from knowing that she was not mentally well."

The pleading for understanding in his tone grated across Juliet's tightly strung nerves. She had a feeling she knew why he'd made her mother leave—because of her affair with Arthur Sinclair.

Words confronting him with that knowledge flew

to the tip of her tongue, but she held back. If the person after her mother had some connection to her father, she wasn't sure telling him what she knew was a good idea. Brandon said she was still in danger. And so was her mother. They had to find her. Quickly.

"She may have had postpartum depression but that doesn't justify your secrets or your lies." Juliet stared at Ronald with tears forming in her eyes and added, "How can we ever trust you again?"

Ronald went to his knees beside Juliet and took her hands. "Believe me, Juliet. I know I betrayed your trust." He looked to all the girls. "All of your trust. If I could undo what I've done, I would. But I can't. Please forgive me."

Never in a million years would Juliet have thought she'd see this man ask for forgiveness. She wasn't sure what to make of such an unexpected turn.

"Our mother is alive," Bianca stated again. "We are going to find her."

Ronald rose and faced her, his eyes harsh. "You do what you must."

He strode from the room.

Bianca sank to the settee. Juliet took her hand and then held her other hand out to Portia. The girls and Winnie followed suit until they had formed a circle.

Juliet closed her eyes. "Dear Lord, bring our

mother home safely. Help each of us to…let go of the past and move forward in Your love," Juliet said aloud. Her heart began to race as the words she'd just said sank in. *Let go of the past.*

Could she let go of what Brandon had done? His motivations for coming to Stoneley hurt deeply. Did she dare trust him, believe he'd planned to tell her the truth? Could she believe his words of love? Her heart wanted to with an intensity that squeezed the breath from her lungs, but her mind wasn't so willing to accept.

All she knew for sure was that the past had destroyed too many lives, hurt too many people. Especially the sisters and aunt she loved so much.

How did she protect them, and herself, from being hurt again?

# FIFTEEN

Ronald closed the door to his study before marching to his desk. The realization of how his actions had so adversely affected his daughters tore at him. He'd been foolish all those years ago to think that removing Trudy from their lives was the best thing for them.

And now one of his daughters had been endangered because of his rashness.

He grabbed the phone and dialed a number he'd hoped never to have to call again. When the line was picked up, he launched into a tirade. "You will pay for trying to hurt my daughter. How dare you think you could get away with this! I'm done. I'm severing our financial agreement, effective immediately. No longer will I support you. You are a menace!"

The voice on the other line whined and complained, but Ronald was done. He slammed down the phone. Emotionally wrung dry, he sunk into his leather captain's chair. From the middle drawer of his desk, he pulled out a photo that he kept hidden in an envelope. The picture showed Trudy on their wedding day. Her green eyes sparkled and her smile showed the promise of their love.

He'd loved her so much. Her betrayal had hurt beyond words.

His foolishness had separated them.

One more regret he had to live with.

Three days later, Winnie blew out a sigh and knocked on Juliet's bedroom door.

"Come in," Juliet called.

Winnie opened the door. Light spilled into the dark room from the hall. Juliet lay on her stomach across her bed. Her hot-pink sweats blended in with the bright flowered comforter. "Juliet, we need to talk."

Juliet rolled over to stare at the ceiling. "Do we have to?"

Winnie smiled slightly, shut the door and went to sit beside her niece. "Yes, we do. Brandon has called repeatedly over the last few days. In fact, he was just on the phone asking for you."

Juliet flung a hand over her eyes, much as she had as a teen when Winnie had come in to "talk" to her about whatever scrape Juliet had managed to get into.

Winnie sighed. "I know about Brandon and his uncle's plans."

Juliet didn't respond.

Winnie moved to lie on her back beside Juliet. Juliet peered at her from beneath her hand.

"I know Brandon hurt and disappointed you."

Juliet snorted.

Winnie hid a smile at the familiar sound. "I felt the same when I first realized why Tate was in town. But then I thought about how anger and bitterness poisons the mind and makes it very sick, much the way the oleander made you sick."

She had Juliet's attention now. Winnie continued, "People make bad choices when their judgment is clouded by anger. I feel a bit sorry for Tate and Brandon. They've both spent so much time and energy hating and hurting that they haven't really lived."

"Have you forgiven Tate, Auntie?"

Winnie thought about that question. "Tate and I have issues that go back further than just the past month. So much damage has been done to his family and to ours by the poisons of revenge and greed."

"And can you get past them?"

Winnie turned to gaze into Juliet's green eyes. "What is it that Shakespeare said? 'Love conquers all.'"

"Uh, Auntie, that was the poet Virgil," Juliet said with a grin.

Winnie waved it off. "Whatever. It sounds like something Shakespeare would have said. But I do know what the Bible says about love. 'Love is the

greatest gift we can give or receive.' First Corinthians chapter thirteen talks about all that love *is*.
One thing that stands out to me in our situation is
that love doesn't count up wrongs and hold them
against others. We all make mistakes, Juliet. I can't
say for sure that Tate and I will have a happily-ever-
after but I am praying we do. I pray that you will
find your happily-ever-after, too."

"With Brandon?"

Winnie shrugged. "That's a question only you
can answer, with God's help. But I do think you
need to give Brandon a chance."

Juliet returned her gaze to the ceiling. "I'm not
ready yet."

Winnie rolled to her side and kissed Juliet's cheek
before standing up. "He showed his dedication to you
by waiting at your bedside, but he won't wait forever."

After a few moments of silence, Winnie left
Juliet's room.

*Can you forgive Tate?*

Winnie searched her heart and found that yes,
she could forgive Tate. He was as much a victim of
the past as the rest of them.

Could she forgive her father and brother? Now
that was a question she struggled with. It would
take time and patience. Fortunately, her love for
Tate was pure.

One question troubled her, though.

Was Tate's love for her pure?

* * *

Juliet remained in her darkened room for a long time as her aunt's words played over in her head. *We all make mistakes. Anger and bitterness poison the mind much the way the oleander made you sick. He showed his dedication to you by waiting at your bedside, but he won't wait forever.*

Her heart ached and her trust had been betrayed. But she couldn't deny that, whatever Brandon's motives, he'd been there for her when she'd needed someone. He hadn't judged her, he hadn't coddled her or felt sorry for her.

*Love doesn't count up wrongs and hold them against others.*

Juliet closed her eyes as more of the passage her aunt quoted came to her. "Love is patient, love is kind. Love is not proud."

A tear slipped from the corner of her eye and left a soggy trail across her cheek.

She did love Brandon, had loved him for a while now. And at the first major bump in the road, she'd bailed. Remorse pushed her own hurt aside.

He'd claimed that he was going to tell her the truth. She never gave him the chance. She'd rashly plunged ahead with her questions and accusations, too confused and impulsive to listen. Acting before thinking, as she had so often throughout her life. She needed to change.

Because she wanted a happily-ever-after with

Brandon. Or at least the opportunity to be happy with him. But she wouldn't have that if she didn't get out of her own way. Her pride had been stung, and yes, her heart bruised. But her spirit was not broken.

She quoted the old Bard as she wiped away her tears. "'The course of true love never did run smooth.'"

For the first two days after Juliet was released from the hospital, Brandon wallowed in regret and a deep sense of loss in his condo while his uncle and Winnie Blanchard were renewing their relationship. Brandon tried not to feel sour that Winnie had forgiven Tate. Brandon was happy for them, he really was. It was just that Juliet wouldn't even talk to him, let alone forgive him.

He and his uncle had dropped their plans to ruin Blanchard Fabrics, which, in retrospect, Brandon realized he hadn't implemented very well. The marketing campaign he and Juliet had worked on was going well. The company was on track to be back in the black. Ronald was pleased. Obviously, Juliet hadn't yet revealed Brandon's and Tate's plan to ruin Blanchard Fabrics, because Ronald had called and demanded Brandon resume his job as soon as possible. That was two days ago.

Brandon had come back to work and found a mindless solidity that helped camouflage the ache of loneliness and regret eating away at his confidence. It would be only a matter of time before he was thrown out. Only a matter of time before there would be no chance to redress the wrong he'd done to Juliet.

Now, sitting at his desk, Brandon called Blanchard Manor for the fifth time and was told the same thing: Juliet was resting and had asked not to be disturbed.

Crestfallen with disappointment, he left Blanchard Fabrics and drew his coat tighter. The late March wind blew in from the ocean, the scent of brine a pungent reminder of the turbulent waters. Above the dusk, clouds were heavy with unspent rain, an ominous sign of the storm to come.

He drove toward his condo. His uncle had said he and Winnie were taking in a movie this evening. They had yet to make their budding romance known to Ronald. Brandon wasn't sure he wanted to be around when they did, not after hearing how Howard and Ronald had broken the couple apart all those years ago.

Tate was having a hard time forgiving the Blanchard men. Though he had agreed to drop their plans for Blanchard Fabrics, Tate's anger toward Ronald and Howard surfaced enough to cause concern. Brandon truly hoped Tate and Winnie would be able to move beyond the past and have a happy life together.

Just as he hoped to do with Juliet. If he could only see her. A flash of loneliness stabbed at him. He banged on the steering wheel. Pain shot into his hand, a welcome relief from the pain gripping his heart.

He drove past his street and headed toward Blanchard Manor. If he showed up on her doorstep, then maybe she'd talk to him. He wasn't going to let her actions stop him. He was determined to plead his case and pray with desperation that she'd soften toward him.

At the gate, he was buzzed in. A good sign, he hoped.

He was greeted at the front door by Miranda. She was an imposing figure in her long skirt and high-necked blouse. Her hair was pulled back and rolled up into a bun like an old-fashioned schoolteacher.

"Good evening, Brandon," she said as she stepped back for him to enter.

Gone were the flowers that had been used to poison Juliet. The large table now supported a huge basket of edible fruit.

"Hello, Miranda. Would you mind seeing if Juliet would come down?"

Miranda hesitated. "I don't know if she will. She's been pretty adamant that she doesn't want to see or talk to you. I don't know what you did to upset her so. We all told her how you saved her life and sat by her bed for hours on end. But she refuses to talk about it."

His stomach dropped and his heart cracked. Now what? "Please tell her I came by. Tell her…tell her I love her."

Miranda's mouth opened and her eyes gleamed. "You do?"

"Very much so."

Miranda narrowed her gaze. "You told her, correct?"

He sighed. "Yes."

"Hmm. Interesting." Miranda looked thoughtful. She opened her mouth to say something just as Winnie came down the stairs. The green, cotton ribbed sweater she wore complimented the color in her hair, which she wore clipped back at the nape of her neck.

"Brandon, it's so good to see you." Winnie gave him a hug. "I'm on my way out."

Miranda tugged on her aunt's arm. "He loves Juliet," she said in a mock whisper.

Winnie patted her hand. "Of course he does, dear. Have you told Juliet he is here?"

"I was just explaining to Brandon that she's been adamant that she doesn't want to see him."

Winnie tucked her arm through Miranda's. "Brandon, why don't you come back tomorrow?"

Recognizing an immovable obstacle when he saw one, Brandon retreated with a polite goodbye, though he wanted to howl with frustration and despair.

He walked back to his car and turned to stare at

the imposing manor house. He remembered that first night he'd come here. He'd been so full of anger and destructive plans that he couldn't have foreseen how much Juliet would come to mean to him. How much it would hurt when she wasn't a part of his life. A suffocating desperation tightened his throat. He had to find a way to see her.

His gaze landed on the path that wound around to the back of the house. An idea formed. He strode to the path and followed it until he stood beneath the balcony of Juliet's room. The French doors leading to the balcony were aglow with light. He searched the ground for several small pebbles. He took aim and launched the first small rock. It bounced on the stone balcony, nowhere near the window. He threw the next three, each hitting his target right on.

He bent to find more stones. Above him he heard the scrape of the French doors opening. He stepped back to see Juliet bathed in light where she stood at the threshold of the doors. A cautious delight tore the breath from his lungs. She was so beautiful. Seeing her made the world seem whole.

"'What light through yonder window breaks?'" he quoted, praying she'd find humor in his attempt to bring her out to talk to him. "'It is the east, and Juliet is the sun. It is my lady, O, it is my love. O, that she knew she were.'"

He heard a suppressed giggle.

"A woman who has captured this horn-beast's soul. I vow upon my honor that my love for thee is true," he continued, improvising. "Let all the evil of this world pass so that I may have a love so sweet as that of Juliet."

A noise somewhere between a moan and a laugh floated on the evening breeze. Then she appeared at the edge of the balcony, wearing a shocking pink sweat suit. Her long braid dangled over her shoulder. "You're nuts! What are you doing?"

"Declaring my undying love," he stated with his hand over his heart.

She hugged herself. "You're going to catch your death of cold out here."

"I have a jacket on." He grinned.

"Well, *I'm* going to catch a cold," she griped with a chuckle.

"Then let me come in. Please, Juliet, we need to talk."

She turned to say something to someone behind her. Great. He had an audience while he made a clown out of himself. He didn't care, not as long as whoever was up there convinced her to let him in.

"Fine. I'll meet you in the living room," she called to him before disappearing back inside.

Tentative relief propelled hope to spiral through him. At least she agreed to see him. Brandon walked back to the front door and knocked. As he waited he sent up a quick prayer. "Lord, You know my heart. Please let Juliet see it, as well."

The door opened. Miranda and Winnie stood there, faces beaming.

Winnie grabbed his arm and pulled him inside. "Quick, before she changes her mind."

Miranda took his coat and hung it on the coatrack.

The two women ushered him to the living room and then quickly left. A moment later Brandon heard Winnie say goodbye to Miranda as she left to meet Tate at the theatre.

Brandon moved to the fireplace and soaked up the warmth from the flames. He watched the orange-and-blue-tinged light's hypnotic dance. Awareness breezed over him. He turned to find Juliet a few feet away.

His heart thumped and bumped against his ribs. His gaze was riveted on her face, then slowly moved over her. She'd changed her clothes, looking lovely in a long, turquoise-blue skirt and cream-colored sweater. Her long hair was now unbound and cascaded over her shoulders in enticing waves.

"You're beautiful," he said.

She gave him a small smile. "Don't think you can come here and charm me into forgiving you."

He took a step forward. "Shoot. There goes my whole strategy."

She matched his step forward. "You'll have to come up with a better one quick."

He took another step, leaving just enough distance for her to make the next move. "How about the truth?"

She stood still, her expression sober and attentive. "That would be good."

"The truth is that you have changed my life. I don't want to be who I was when I came to Stoneley. I want to be the man you brought out in me. A man who loves you and who wants to spend the rest of his life making you happy."

He held his breath as she studied him. He tried to put in his expression all the love overflowing in his heart.

"Do you know what the Bible says about love?"

He shook his head.

She closed the distance between them and laid a hand over his heart. He sucked in a breath, but remained still despite every instinct in him screaming to wrap her in his arms and never let go.

"'Love is the greatest gift.'"

Her softly spoken words knocked the wind from his lungs. "Is this a gift I can ever hope to receive from you?"

"You know it won't be easy. Our families have a lot of bad history."

"But that doesn't have to be our future," he managed to say.

"There's still so much unresolved with my mother and…Sinclair."

He placed his hand over hers. "I'll be with you the whole way."

"It could get ugly."

Leaning his forehead against hers, he whispered, "Not as long as we're together."

She shifted her head and gazed into his eyes. "Don't keep secrets from me again."

"I wouldn't dream of it."

A joyous smile spread over her face. "Then kiss me and seal our future."

He arched an eyebrow. "Ah, but, fair maid, have thee no words of love for me?"

Her green eyes gleamed. "Three words, I do have."

"Then put me out of my misery and say them!"

She slid her arm around his neck and pulled him close so their noses touched. *"I love you."*

"Hallelujah," he murmured before he wrapped his arms around his beloved enemy and sealed their future with a kiss.

"Next in line," called the airline ticket agent.

A woman stepped forward, her hand going to the yellow scarf covering her blond hair. She adjusted the big, black sunglasses covering half her petite face as she stated, "I need a one-way ticket to Maine."

\* \* \* \* \*

Dear Reader,

Thank you for joining Juliet Blanchard in her quest to help find her mother. Though the mystery of THE SECRETS OF STONELEY continues, Juliet discovered something more precious than the answers she sought: she found love.

As Aunt Winnie pointed out to Juliet, love is the greatest gift.

When reading the passage about love in 1 Corinthians 13, I'm struck by several things. Love is more than tingling sensations that heat the blood and make us feel euphoric. Love is active. It takes effort on our part to love. We put the well-being of those we love ahead of our own, we work toward unity and we treat our loved ones with respect and concern. Through the Bible, God shows us what love is, what love does. I challenge you to read the hundreds of passages in God's Word that teach us how to love and receive love.

May you find love overflowing through Him who loves you,

# QUESTIONS FOR DISCUSSION

1. Have you read THE SECRETS OF STONELEY series from the beginning? If so, what made you start the series? If not, will you go back and read the series from beginning to end?

2. Juliet is the "baby" of the family. Where do you fall in your family? Are you an only child? Do you have brothers or sisters or both? If you are the youngest, is your relationship with your siblings similar to that of the Blanchard sisters? Do you feel as though you don't get taken seriously?

3. Of all the characters in the story, which one did you identify most with? Why?

4. Did the reunion between Winnie and Tate add to the story? Did you see parallels in the two romances?

5. Was there enough suspense and mystery to keep you guessing? How so?

6. What lessons of love did you learn from this story? What Scripture passages were brought to mind as you read Juliet and Brandon's story?

7. What did you think of the Shakespearean references? Did you like the balcony scene in this story? Did you think there should have been more or less Shakespearean references?

8. Brandon and Tate had plans for revenge. Do you think that taking revenge is productive? How do you handle the hurts in your life? Does hardening your heart help or harm?

9. Juliet and Brandon both found peace within the walls of a church. Do you believe that only in a church can you find God? Where else do you feel His presence?

10. Juliet came home to work at Blanchard Fabrics to try to get closer to her father, putting her own dreams of fashion designing on hold. Have you ever put a dream on hold for someone else? How did you feel about it? Did you ever try to fulfill your dream at a later date, or did your dream change?

*Rissa Blanchard feared that, like her long-lost
mother, she was losing her mind.
And someone seemed to be helping her along.
Could Detective Drew Lancaster save
her from the edge of madness?
Find out in Irene Brand's
THE SOUND OF SECRETS.*

*And now, turn the page for a sneak preview of
THE SOUND OF SECRETS,
the fourth installment of*
THE SECRETS OF STONELEY.
*On sale in April 2007 from Steeple Hill Books.*

Drew had just returned to the library and settled into a chair when Rissa's scream brought him to his feet. He'd noticed that she hadn't gone to bed when her twin had, but he thought she might have gone upstairs while he was checking the rest of the house. A light was still on in the living room and he headed in that direction.

He looked in the half-open door before Rissa knew he was there. He felt bad for her when he saw she was trembling and rocking back and forth in agony. Feeling like a spy, he knocked softly.

Rissa lifted her head like a startled fawn.

"Are you all right?"

She shook her head.

"Is it all right for me to come in?"

She closed her eyes and nodded. He knelt on the floor beside her.

In a quiet voice, she whispered, "Did you hear a woman crying?"

"I heard someone scream here in the library. I thought it was you."

"Oh, no, it wasn't me," she protested. "It came from far away. Please say it wasn't me."

Puzzled by her distress and the wild look in her eyes, he hastened to say, "I heard a scream, but I'm not sure where it came from. Maybe you cried out in your sleep. You've had enough stress tonight to cause nightmares, finding your mother's body."

Shaking her head back and forth, tears slid over her pale cheeks and she trembled. Without considering the propriety of his actions, Drew sat beside her on the settee and pulled her into a soft, impersonal embrace. He half expected a rebuff, but after a few minutes, Rissa became quiet.

Rissa had never felt so secure, but still she wondered if it was wise for her to take comfort in Drew's embrace. After the emotional stress she'd been under all evening, Rissa allowed herself the luxury of feeling protected. Forgetting the woman's cry for a moment, Rissa now had a slight understanding of why Portia was so eager to marry Mick. She had never doubted before that her career was all she needed in life, but now she questioned if she was missing something vitally important.

She hadn't envied Portia's apparent happiness because her twin wanted what marriage would bring. She loved children and was eagerly looking forward to becoming Kaitlyn's stepmother. But Portia would make a good wife and mother. Rissa wouldn't. Her twin had apparently gotten all of the maternal instincts that should have been divided between them. She couldn't imagine herself as a mother, and she believed most men wanted children, especially a son. Would anyone want to marry her if she didn't want to start a family?

Hoping to calm her, Drew tried to think of something to talk about that would take her mind off of the nightmare. He kept his arm around her, but pulled away slightly so he could look into her face.

"Rissa," he said contemplatively. "I don't believe I've known anyone else who had that name.

The uneasiness left her eyes and was replaced by a nostalgic expression. "Unless you're a student of Shakespeare, I don't suppose you would have heard the name."

"You've lost me there, ma'am. I've heard of Shakespeare, but I've never read any of his stuff."

Rissa sighed. "My sisters and I learned about Shakespeare's works before we studied our ABCs, I think. All of us were named for characters in his works. We have most of them on our library shelves."

Drew's reading was pretty much limited to *National Geographic* and hobby magazines. He knew that Shakespeare had lived in England hundreds of years ago but that was it! He couldn't imagine why anyone would be so wrapped up in ancient literature that they would name their children after the characters.

"I don't know why, but my mother and maybe my father, too, were Shakespeare enthusiasts. I won't bore you with all the details, but our oldest sister, Miranda, her name came from *The Tempest*. My next sister, Bianca, was named after a character in *The Taming of the Shrew*. Cordelia's name was taken from *King Lear*, although we've always called her Delia. Portia and Nerissa were characters in *The Merchant of Venice*. And surely you've heard of *Romeo and Juliet*—that's where our baby sister, Juliet, got her name."

Drew shook his head in disbelief and stared at her intently. "I remember being introduced to Shakespeare's work in English Literature during my high school years, but I haven't given him a thought since." He shrugged dismissively. "Unbelievable, to me, that anybody in today's world would still be interested."

"If you ever come to the city, I'd like to take you to see a production of one of Shakespeare's plays. You'd really enjoy it."

Noting the skeptical expression in his eyes, Rissa knew she hadn't convinced him.

"Are you settled down enough now to go upstairs to bed?" Drew asked softly. "It's still a few hours until daylight."

Sighing, she moved away from the comfort of his arms.

"I'll stay here the rest of the night," she said. "If I go to our room, I'd wake Portia. I'll try to sleep, but the nightmare is still vivid in my mind. I'm convinced that I heard a woman's cry. I haven't been sleeping well for several months, but I've never had this happen before. Thanks for helping, Drew."

He stood awkwardly. Knowing that he had been excused, he would have to leave, but considering the tension on her face, he wasn't sure she should stay alone.

"I'll be across the hall if you need me, but try to sleep. Nothing's going to happen with me on guard. I'll see you in the morning."

# REQUEST YOUR FREE BOOKS!

## 2 FREE INSPIRATIONAL NOVELS
## PLUS 2
## FREE
## MYSTERY GIFTS

*Love Inspired*

**YES!** Please send me 2 FREE Love Inspired® novels and my 2 FREE mystery gifts. After receiving them, if I don't wish to receive any more books, I can return the shipping statement marked "cancel." If I don't cancel, I will receive 4 brand-new novels every month and be billed just $3.99 per book in the U.S., or $4.74 per book in Canada, plus 25¢ shipping and handling per book and applicable taxes, if any*. That's a savings of 20% off the cover price! I understand that accepting the 2 free books and gifts places me under no obligation to buy anything. I can always return a shipment and cancel at any time. Even if I never buy another book from Steeple Hill, the two free books and gifts are mine to keep forever.

113 IDN EF26   313 IDN EF27

| Name | (PLEASE PRINT) | |
|---|---|---|
| Address | | Apt. # |
| City | State/Prov. | Zip/Postal Code |

Signature (if under 18, a parent or guardian must sign)

### Order online at www.LoveInspiredBooks.com

### Or mail to Steeple Hill Reader Service™:

**IN U.S.A.:** P.O. Box 1867, Buffalo, NY 14240-1867
**IN CANADA:** P.O. Box 609, Fort Erie, Ontario  L2A 5X3

Not valid to current Love Inspired subscribers.

### Want to try two free books from another series?
### Call 1-800-873-8635 or visit www.morefreebooks.com

* Terms and prices subject to change without notice. NY residents add applicable sales tax. Canadian residents will be charged applicable provincial taxes and GST. This offer is limited to one order per household. All orders subject to approval. Credit or debit balances in a customer's account(s) may be offset by any other outstanding balance owed by or to the customer. Please allow 4 to 6 weeks for delivery.

LIREG07